BACK TO THE OLD WEST

A TIME TRAVEL ROMANCE

LOVE THROUGHOUT TIME
BOOK TEN

ID JOHNSON

For Bessie

CONTENTS

1

CHEATED

Granddad Hank deals the cards like he's done every Saturday, and every shuffle carries a memory of all the Saturdays before. The cards are worn smooth, with edges softened by generations of hands that have held them tight. Grandad calls this version *Frontier Poker*, which is nothing like Texas Hold'em. When the Rawlins men play, there are no blinds and no fancy tricks. There's just five cards, an ante, and the kind of grit a cowboy brings to the table, the way cards were played it in saloons in the old days.

On Saturdays, if we don't have other plans, the house fills up for dinner and poker at my grandparents' place. We've just finished eating, and from the other room comes the sound of laughter. Grandma Rita, my mom, and my aunts are drinking wine. My dad sits across the poker table with two of his brothers, and my cousin Eli sits on the other side with me. Granddad Hank sits at the head of the table and pushes the last card of my hand across.

I glance down at the cards in front of me but don't reach for them right away. I keep thinking about how Marissa cheated on me, lied, and didn't even act like she was sorry. My mind keeps replaying walking in on her with another guy, and I just can't let those images go.

So I came over to my grandparents' place to get my mind off Marissa. I haven't said a word about the breakup, and nobody's asked. In this family, we don't have to spill our guts to be welcomed in. We just show up and take our usual seats.

I finally look at my cards. It's a strong hand, solid enough to work with. Dad tosses in his ante and eyes me like he's trying to read something in my face. I keep my expression neutral. Years of EMT calls taught me how to steady my hands, breath, and voice, even when everything is going to hell around me.

Eli pushes chips into the middle of the table. I follow, and the game rolls on. Cards move, bets go in, and the table fills with the usual intense focus.

I stay in and raise a modest amount, trying to keep my mind on the cards, but my thoughts keep wandering back to how much I loved Marissa, and how, even though I gave her my all, she still cheated. The warning signs were there, and I missed them because I was working so hard and trying to provide a life for her.

Grandad Hank meets my raise, barely lifting an eyebrow, and Eli stays in, too, overconfident as usual. When it comes down to the final play, it's just the three of us. Grandad studies his cards, studies me, then folds with a grunt that means I've passed whatever test he set.

Eli tries to stare me down, but it doesn't work. I've held pressure on a man with a gunshot wound in the back of an ambulance while being shot at through the rig, without flinching. My cousin with his weak poker face isn't going to shake me.

He flips over a pair of sevens with a triumphant grin. I lay my cards down slowly, a pair of jacks. His frown tells me he knows he's been outplayed again. The win is clean.

Everyone in the room groans but then laughs. Grandad slaps the table, proud of me. Dad shakes his head, smiling. "Of course you win, Jake. You never lose."

Their noise fills the room, and I find myself smiling, not because I won, but because I'm here, surrounded by family.

After the last hand, I step onto the porch, and Eli follows with two beers in hand. We've been friends since we were kids–cousins, but closer than most brothers I know. He hands me a beer and then leans his shoulder against the post, giving me a look I know he's been holding in since the second I sat down at the dinner table.

"All right," he says, taking a drink. "Why are you here tonight? As soon as you walked in, I knew I wasn't winning a single damn hand. I had been winning a few rounds since you're usually out with Marissa on Saturdays."

I sit in the rocking chair and let the beer bottle rest on my knee. "Yeah, well, we definitely didn't have a date tonight."

His eyebrows lift. "Did something happen?"

"Yes," I say quietly. "She ended it."

Eli's eyes narrow the way they do when he's deciding whether to say something or just let me be.

"She cheated." There's no reason for me to dress it up. It's the truth, and saying it plainly doesn't hurt any more or any less.

Eli shakes his head. "Damn, Jake. I'm sorry."

I take a long drink. "I walked in on them. Came home from work early, and you know what? I didn't even see it coming."

"Hell," he murmurs. "No wonder you showed up ready to wipe the floor with us. You needed a win."

"I definitely needed something," I say. "Wasn't gonna sit in that apartment staring at the walls. Four years of my life, down the shitter."

He nods and takes a sip of his beer. "Do you remember the quail hunting trip we took to the Rio Grande?"

It's a sharp turn of conversation, but not unwelcome. "Of course I remember. It's hard to forget a beautiful piece of land like that. That was one of the best quail hunts we've ever had."

"I've been thinking about it lately," he says. "That ridge we hunted at sunrise on Logan's uncle's land, and the way the dogs found so many coveys. It was unreal. The only sounds we heard all morning were gunshots and the rushing river."

I nod, the memory easing my broken heart just a little.

He glances at me. "We should go back next weekend."

"Oh? Why's that?" I keep my tone even, but the idea hits like fresh air after being underwater too long.

"It would be good for us all. Come on. Next weekend. Me, you, Tate, Logan, and Ryan. No women. No schedules. No city noise. Just us, our bird dogs, a campfire, and the kind of peace you need."

That last part sinks deep. A weekend out by the river, the timberline, cold streams, nothing but space and sky, would be the first real peace I've had in days.

"I could use a weekend like that," I admit.

"I figured." He tips his bottle toward me.

"All right," I say, clinking my bottle with his. "Let's do it."

Eli grins. "Good. I'll call the guys in the morning."

For the first time since Marissa left, I'm actually looking forward to something again.

* * *

We roll out of Houston before sunrise, our trucks packed with gear, rifles, and enough supplies to last the weekend. My black-and-white German Shorthaired Pointer, Ace, rides in his kennel in the bed of my truck. I've had him since he was a pup, and he's been on more hunting trips than I can count.

Eli rides shotgun, with Logan in back, their dogs kenneled next to mine. Tate and Ryan follow in the second truck, their dogs and gear stacked high, coolers and packs wedged in around the kennels.

Every inch of both trucks is full: rifles locked in racks, camp chairs, tarps, sleeping bags, ice chests, backpacks loaded with water and snacks, and extra ammo for good measure.

We push through Texas the first day, the flat land rolling by in endless shades of brown and gold. The trucks hum along the highways, carrying us past small towns and empty stretches of road. We only stop for fuel, a quick bite, and to stretch the dogs' legs.

By late evening, the terrain starts to open as we near Mesilla. New Mexico's scrub brush gives way to the wide, golden fields of the Rio

Grande Valley. Dusty bushes and mesquite line the roadside, which are the perfect cover for quail. We pull off onto a flat stretch of Logan's uncle's land beside the river, clouds of dust rising from the road. Logan jumps out first, letting the dogs out to run and sniff the air. Eli and I start unloading rifles, backpacks, coolers, kennels, chairs, and tents. Tate and Ryan pull in behind us, moving with the same efficiency.

Ace is already circling, his nose twitching and his tail wagging. I sling my pack over my shoulder, take a deep breath, and let the tension in my chest ease. The Rio Grande glimmers in the moonlight, the brush along the banks perfect for flushing birds.

We feed and water our dogs, stake tents, stretch tarps, grab beers and snacks from our coolers, and set up our chairs.

"Man, Ace is something else," Eli says, watching him nose around. "Remember that guided hunt up in Nebraska? Those guys wanted to buy him off you on the spot."

I laugh, shaking my head. "Yeah. They saw him point a covey one hundred yards away, steady as a statue. Then they tried to lowball me for him."

Logan whistles. "You nearly decked the guy, didn't you? I saw it in your eyes."

"Almost," I admit. "I told him in no uncertain terms that Ace isn't for sale."

Ryan grins, leaning on the tailgate. "Speaking of decking a guy, remember that night at the bar in Austin?"

I shake my head. "Yes. Some idiot thought it was funny to slap Marissa on the ass." My jaw tightens a little instinctually, but I keep my voice calm. "He didn't know who he was dealing with. I taught him some manners, right there on the floor."

Ryan laughs. "I knew better than to get between you and anyone dumb enough to touch your girl."

I shrug, letting it slide. That was then. This is now. And at the moment, I don't have a girl.

We grab sandwiches and more cold beers from the coolers and settle into the camp chairs. The conversation bounces around from inside jokes about past hunts to a challenge over who gets the last slice of salami. Laughter cuts through the quiet evening, and for a while, I almost forget about my problems.

Then, we notice the sky starting to change in the west. Dark clouds blot out the moon for a moment. Eli points upward. "That storm looks like it's coming in fast. We should get everything squared away before it hits."

"Yeah," Tate agrees, already grabbing coolers and rifles. "Better move everything into tents or trucks."

We all split up, hauling chairs, backpacks, and rifles under cover. The dogs circle and sniff the edges of the camp one last time, enjoying the cooler air before the rain hits.

I toss my backpack inside the tent, and Ace runs inside, too. He calms down immediately, curling up on the small blanket I brought him. I duck inside, and the first raindrops hit the nylon just as I zip the flap closed.

Crawling inside the tent, I unroll my sleeping bag. The canvas rattles with each clap of thunder. I lie back, listening. "Wow... that was close, huh?" I say to Ace.

The next instant, fire rips through my right leg. Muscle and bone feel like they're being torn apart. I scream, clutching the pole as my body convulses violently. White-hot agony flashes through me. My chest hammers, limbs thrash, and then I black out.

When I wake, pain sears my right leg, and every breath I take is excruciating. I realize I've been struck by lightning, and somehow, I'm still alive.

Ace nudges my side, a low whine in his throat. I roll onto my hands and knees, forcing my right leg to move with me, each motion sending sharp pain shooting through it and down to my foot.

I push the tent flap aside and stumble into the moonlit clearing, dragging my leg. The camp's gone. Our trucks, dogs, tents, and everyone else, all of them, are just gone.

I stare at the empty sand and brush, the Rio glinting in the distance, and start to wonder what the hell is happening. Maybe a tornado carried everything and everyone away while I was uncon-scious, but then why are Ace and I still here?

I test the leg with another drag-step; raw pain shoots up my thigh and knee. I check my gear: backpack on, rifle in the tent, and my phone is in my pocket. Ace stays tight at my side, alert and tense.

I drag myself forward, scanning the horizon. I hear cattle nearby.

"Eli!" I yell.

I listen, but there's no reply. Then I realize I don't hear the hum of the highway in the distance. At first, I think I just can't hear it, but then I look, and there is no outer road at all. There's no asphalt and nothing but sagebrush where it should be.

I squat, gripping Ace's collar, trying to catch my breath. "What the hell, Ace? Where the fuck is everybody?"

2

———

STRANGE FELLOW

Thunder splits the sky so close it rattles my bones, the sound rolling over the land like some kind of monster. Rain lashes down in hard, slanted sheets, driven sideways by the wind, soaking me through in seconds. Chaco shifts beneath me, uneasy, his ears flicking back as lightning flashes again, turning the world stark white for a heartbeat before plunging it back into darkness.

"Easy," I murmur, leaning forward, running one hand over his mane.

The goats are everywhere, scattered shapes moving in panicked bursts, bleating sharp and wild as the storm bears down on us. They don't understand thunder. They don't understand lightning. They only know fear, and fear makes them run in all the wrong directions.

"Go on," I call to the dogs, raising my voice over the wind. Margot darts left, Huck swings wide, and Lady streaks ahead, all three of them soaked and slick with rain but moving fast, instincts sharp even in the chaos. I guide Chaco toward the far fence line, trying to funnel the goats back toward the barn, my heart pounding harder with every flash of lightning.

Another thunderclap cracks so loud it feels like the sky has split open. Chaco spooks, jumping sideways, and I nearly lose my seat. I clamp my legs down, my breath tearing out of me.

"Don't," I whisper. "Please don't."

The barn looms ahead, a dark shape barely visible through the rain, its doors yawning open with a promise of safety. If I can just get them inside…. If I can just keep everyone moving….

Lightning strikes again, and this time, it hits far too close. A blinding flash explodes to my right, followed by a sound like the earth itself snapping in half. Heat washes over me an instant later. I turn just in time to see a tree near the yard erupt, flames licking up its trunk even as rain pours down around it.

"Oh, God! Help me!"

Fire and water at the same time. Wind whipping sparks sideways. The goats scatter again, shrieking, bolting away from the sudden light and noise. One breaks toward the burning tree, and my chest tightens painfully.

"No, no, no!"

I dig my heels in, turning Chaco hard, shouting to the dogs. Margot veers instantly, cutting the goat off. Huck skids in the mud, nearly goes down, and scrambles back up. Lady snaps and darts, driving the herd back together by inches.

Another gust of wind tears through the pasture, nearly ripping me sideways out of the saddle. Branches whip overhead. Something cracks and falls behind us, heavy enough to make the ground shudder.

This is stupid! a voice in my head screams. This is how people get killed, but the goats are still out here, and they're my responsibility. I'm the only one standing between them and real danger.

Lightning flashes again, so bright it turns the rain into needles of silver. For a split second, I see everything: the goats' wide eyes, the churned mud, the fire chewing its way up the tree, and then just as quickly, darkness slams back around.

My hands shake on the reins. I wish—God, I wish—there were someone here to help me.

I wish there were someone to ride the far side, to watch my back, and to shout over the storm and tell me where to go next when I'm not sure of which direction is best. I swallow hard, my throat burning, and push the thought away because wishing doesn't get goats into barns.

"Go!" I shout, my voice raw. "Move!"

We drive them forward in a ragged wave. One by one, then two, then three at a time, the goats funnel into the barn, hooves clattering on wood, bodies pressing together in terrified relief. I don't breathe properly until the last one disappears inside.

Another thunderclap booms overhead. Chaco sidesteps again, his muscles tight and his sides heaving. I slide down from the saddle on unsteady legs, splashing into mud, and slam the barn doors shut with all my strength. The sound echoes, final and solid.

For a moment, I just stand there in the dark, rain plastering my hair to my face, chest rising and falling too fast. The dogs crowd close, wet bodies pressing into my legs, seeking reassurance I barely have to give.

"You're okay," I whisper, more to myself than to them. "We're okay."

But the words don't feel entirely true. I lean my forehead against the barn door. I miss my mother tonight. I miss her calm voice and the way she always knew what to do when things went wrong. I miss my father, and the certainty that nothing could touch me if he was nearby.

The storm rages on, lightning flashing, thunder rolling, the fire in the tree being washed away by the rain. Standing here in the dark, soaked and shaking, I feel how lonely this life can be and how heavy it is to carry everything myself.

I straighten slowly, wiping rain from my face. At least now the animals are safe. That has to be enough for tonight.

But as another bolt of lightning splits the sky, I can't help wishing, just for tonight, that I didn't have to face storms like this alone.

* * *

MORNING LIGHT RIPPLES OVER THE JORNADA LIKE A BLESSING I'M NOT sure I deserve. It's thin and pale, more gold than gray, but it's enough to make even the dust shimmer as I ride the fence line with my three dogs loping ahead, marveling at how quickly the desert sun can dry up the mud and turn it into powdery dirt. Margot runs closest, her black ears bouncing with each stride, glancing back every few seconds to make sure I'm still there like she always does. I swear that dog can always tell when I'm worried.

I dismount Chaco at the first broken stretch of fence. The storm last night with its crazy wind must've loosened the rails, or it could've been a stubborn steer leaning too hard. Either way, it's another thing to fix and another chore that steals time I don't have. My gloves scrape against the rough cedar posts as I lift the splintered rail into place, the wood heavy in my arms. My fingers ache from gripping it, and my shoulders burn from lifting and nailing it back into place. Every minute spent here is a minute I'm not checking the cattle, patching another hole, or trying to figure out how to raise the money I owe for supplies and taxes.

The sun rises higher, and my shirt clings to my back with sweat by the time I get the fence mended. I straighten and watch a lone buzzard circle overhead. "I'm working on it," I mutter to the sky, though I doubt God or the birds give a damn that I owe money to half the valley.

I think about the supplies from town and the cattle doctor's tinctures I still owe money for. I think about the property taxes, which are so high it feels as if the government wants to drive every rancher off the land. I go over the numbers in my head again and again as I walk back to my horse, and each sum seems higher than the last, pressing down on my shoulders and making me tired before I even swing back into the saddle.

Margot sits beside Chaco, her tongue out, looking up at me. She nudges my leg with her nose like she can push comfort into me.

"I know, ol' girl," I say, reaching down and rubbing her head. "Worrying won't fix a fence or pay a debt, will it?"

We keep moving. There's always another post leaning, another stretch sagging. Huck and Lady trail after a jackrabbit, disappearing and reappearing in the brush, their tails wagging. But Margot stays glued to me. She's the best dog I've ever trained and the best companion I've ever had.

By midday, my shoulders ache, and dirt cakes my face, throat, and arms. All morning, I've been thinking I should sell off a few acres. After all, pride won't save the ranch, and neither will memories.

My father's voice seems to follow me everywhere I go. "A rancher holds what they can and fights for the rest." He's been gone for years, but I still hear his words, and I know he's right.

I pause at the top of a rise overlooking the valley. Far in the distance, sits Mesilla a far off shimmer, blurred by the heat. Then, Margot pricks her ears, and before I can ask what she sees, she takes off down the slope. She barks sharply, one of her warning calls, but not the panicked kind. She sounds more curious than alarmed, and Huck and Lady race after her, yipping.

"Margot!" I call, but she's gone, swallowed by mesquite and sunbaked scrub.

A minute later, Margot trots toward me proudly, tail high, guiding a black-and-white dog unlike any I've ever seen. He isn't skinny or weathered; his coat is sleek, and his frame is lean and athletic in a way that doesn't match any ranch dog or hound around these parts. There's a refined look to him, as if he were bred for a purpose I can't quite name, and his eyes move over the land with a sharp, intelligent focus that feels out of place in this dusty country.

Margot nudges him forward with the easy confidence of a dog introducing a friend she trusts. The newcomer steps closer, studying me with curiosity rather than fear.

I dismount and take one slow step toward the strange dog, but he turns before I can reach out a hand. Without hesitation, he pads back the way he came, glancing over his shoulder as if making sure I'm following. Margot gives a short bark and trots after him, so I jump back on Chaco and move downhill through the brush.

The dog leads with purpose, weaving through tall brush and creosote bushes, pausing only long enough to make sure I'm still behind him.

The sun grows hotter on my shoulders as we descend into a shallow swale tucked between two rocky ridges. At first, I don't see anything unusual. Then, I spot a splash of red against the brown and green. A man in a red shirt lies half-hidden in the shade of a cedar, stretched out on his back like he was simply dropped from the sky.

I stop short.

He's young, maybe near my age, with a handsome face, and sandy brown hair cut short by a hand more skilled than anyone I know in these parts. His clothes are even more strange than his dog. The fabric looks sturdy but woven tight and smooth, not wool or rough cotton. His boots have a shine to them I've never seen on working leather. Beside him on the ground sits a pack made of some material I can't name, with buckles and stitching too precise to be done by hand, but it's the rifle that steals my breath.

The metal gleams unnaturally bright in the sunlight. The barrel is sleek, without the usual heaviness of wear, and the stock is shaped with a precision no gunsmith I know could produce. It looks new in a way nothing stays new out here. Not for long. Not with this dust and heat.

"What in God's name..." I whisper.

Margot approaches the man carefully, sniffing his hand, her tail giving a cautious wag. The black and white dog sits beside his shoulder, his posture protective but calm, as if guarding him.

I kneel a couple of feet away and see his chest moving. *Well, he's alive, then.* I notice his face is attractive in a way that makes me look twice, even with his eyes closed. One sleeve is torn, and there's dried blood along his right leg, but it's not enough to explain why he's sprawled senseless out here in the middle of nowhere.

I reach toward his shoulder, meaning to shake him awake, fingers hovering just above his shirt, but something in my gut screams caution.

A man with strange clothes, an even stranger rifle, and a dog like this one didn't walk here from town. He didn't come from any ranch I know, and if he wakes confused, injured, and dangerous, I don't want to be alone with him when he does.

I stand slowly, brushing sand off my hands. "All right," I say to Margot, though my voice is barely above a whisper. "We'll go get help."

Andy might complain, but he's strong, level-headed, and good with strangers.

I take one last look at the unconscious man, mount my horse, and turn Chaco back toward the rise, gathering Margot, Huck, and Lady with a sharp whistle. The strange black and white dog follows us, too.

I ride hard back toward the ranch, the dogs pacing at my horse's heels. Andy is in the barn, mending tack, when I pull up short enough to kick soil over his boots.

He squints up at me. "You look like you've seen a ghost."

"Not a ghost," I say, short of breath, "but something close. I need your help."

Andy doesn't ask questions. He grabs his rifle, swings onto his mare, and falls in beside me as I turn back toward the ridge. "All right," he says finally, nudging his horse up to a trot. "Tell me what's happened, and who's this dog?"

"There's a man out here on Sawyer land. He's hurt, has on bright clothes I've never seen, and a very strange-looking rifle."

By the time we crest the slope again, I can see the cedar where the man's lying, but he's no longer unconscious.

He's awake, seated against the trunk, drinking from a canteen unlike any I've ever known. His wounded leg is wrapped tightly in white bandages that look clean and evenly cut, nothing like the rough cloth strips we keep in the tack room. His strange pack is on his back, his arms looped through its straps.

Margot reaches him first, tail wagging, and the stranger's dog trots proudly at her side. The man looks up as Andy and I approach.

"You found help," he murmurs to his dog and then turns his attention to us. "Howdy. My name's Jake Rawlins, and this here is Ace."

I swallow, suddenly aware of how grimy and windblown I must look. "I'm Joanna Calloway," I say. "This is my friend Andy."

Jake nods politely, but his eyes dart around, taking in the land, the dogs, and the horses, as if trying to make sense of it all.

I clear my throat. "Are you a family member or friend of Chase Sawyer?"

Jake shakes his head. "No, ma'am. Don't know the name."

"Well," I say, an uneasy prickle working down my spine, "you're on his land."

Jake looks confused. "I… don't know how I got here." His hand tightens around the strange canteen. "I was out camping with my friends when a storm blew up fast. Lightning struck near us." He gestures to the bandage. "I think my leg got struck by lightning. Then everything went white. When I woke up, my friends, their dogs, and our camp were gone. I've been walking all night. Must've passed out."

Andy and I exchange a sideways glance. Getting struck by lightning could kill a man. This Jake Rawlins must be a tough ol' boy.

"You're in no shape to stay out here," I say. "You need to rest, and we need to take a better look at that leg."

Jake hesitates but then nods. "I'd appreciate that very much, if you don't mind."

Andy dismounts and hands over his reins. "Go on. You can ride my horse. You know how to ride?"

Jake nods, gathers his belongings, and then climbs into the saddle awkwardly, wincing but managing to mount. Ace circles once, then falls into step beside him as naturally as if he's done it a thousand times.

Andy climbs onto Chaco behind me, and I lead the way, the dogs trotting behind, the three of us and two horses moving slowly down the trail toward home.

When we reach my house, I guide Jake into the spare room, keeping one hand near his elbow in case his injured leg gives out. Andy stays close behind us, ready to help if I need it, but Jake forces himself forward with a stubbornness that makes me think he's used to pushing through pain. I pull the quilt back and gesture for him to sit. The moment he lowers himself onto the mattress, he mumbles a soft thank you, his eyes already heavy, and before I can tell him he's welcome to rest as long as he needs, he's already drifting back to sleep.

Ace slips into the room a moment later, his claws clacking against the floorboards. He noses at the side of the bed, checking on his partner with a quiet, worried whine. I crouch beside him and stroke the fur between his ears. "Come on, boy," I murmur, guiding him gently toward the door so Jake can sleep.

His dog follows me to the kitchen, where I fill a bowl with water and set it in front of him. He drinks as I put some dog scraps into another dish, and as he eats, my dogs approach, cautious but curious. They know Ace isn't a threat.

Andy leans against the counter, his hat in his hands, turning it in slow circles. I can tell he's trying to decide how to phrase whatever he's thinking. "So," he says finally, "that's a strange fellow. I wonder where he's from."

"I guess we'll find out when he wakes up."

Andy nods but doesn't look reassured. "You believe what he said? That he and his friends made camp, and he got hit by lightning? Which made his friends disappear? Joanna... his clothes... and that rifle—I've never seen a rifle like that. And that damn bag of his has more straps than a harness."

"I know," I say quietly. "But I don't think he's lying. Whatever happened out there, he's confused—and maybe a little scared. He tried to hide it, but I could tell."

Andy studies me for a long moment, the way he does when he's weighing all the possibilities. "People who are confused and scared can be trouble," he says, not accusingly, just stating the truth we both know.

"I'm aware," I tell him. "We'll keep an eye on him. If he turns out to be a problem, we'll deal with it, but I'm not turning away a man who can barely keep his eyes open."

He hesitates and then nods. "All right. I'll stay close by. Yell if anything feels off."

"I will," I promise.

The screen door shuts behind him, and I stay in the kitchen, glancing toward the spare room. Mr. Rawlins is asleep, but I can't stop thinking about him. Who is he, and how did he end up here?

3

———————

1875

I wake in a borrowed bed and sit up slowly. Ace lies asleep on the floor, and there's a plate of food and a glass of water on the side table. My leg hurts, but it's nothing I can't handle. I swing my feet off the bed and test my weight.

Stepping toward the window, I pull back the curtain and look outside. The sun is already sinking over the horizon, like I've been sleeping all day.

A ranch stretches out in front of me: barns, horses grazing, and hundreds of cattle scattered across the land. It looks like something out of an old photograph from the late 1800s, but without the wear and tear of a century. Nothing modern stands out to me—no trucks, horse trailers, tractors, or machinery. Not even a telephone pole. Just a wide, open space with animals, fences, and wooden buildings.

I squint. Maybe this is some kind of reenactment or a museum. It wouldn't be the first place like that I've seen.

A knock on the door interrupts my thoughts. "Come in," I call.

The woman from yesterday steps in. Joanna, I think? "How's your leg?" she asks. Her smile is kind, her green eyes twinkling with a curiosity that reaches beyond her simple question. Long blonde hair is wound up in a bun on top of her head, and when she smiles, her face somehow becomes even more beautiful.

"My leg hurts," I admit, limping a little as I move in her direction. "But it'll be fine. Thanks for giving me a place to rest."

She nods and gestures toward the door. "I was thinking we could go into the kitchen for a bit and talk a little."

I follow her down the hall, and Ace stays close beside me. In the kitchen, she pours two glasses of whiskey and hands me one. I glance at the bottle. *1874.*

"This is some incredibly old whiskey," I mutter. "Where'd you get it?"

She looks at the bottle and then back at me, a little confused. "Old? It's from last year."

I pause. The ranch, the whiskey, Joanna's clothes….

My pulse quickens as reality sinks in. This isn't a museum. This isn't some movie set. Somehow, the storm threw me back in time. I'm in 1875.

I take a deep breath, trying to calm myself, and sit down at the table. I take a sip from the glass, and the confusion intensifies. *1875.* I keep turning the number over and over in my head, like it's a riddle I can't crack.

Joanna sits across from me, watching me carefully, waiting for me to say something, but there's nothing to say. Nothing that makes sense. How could this be real?

"Are you all right?" Joanna asks.

I nod, though I'm far from it. "Uh… yes, I will be. I hope."

She tilts her head, looking at me like she's trying to gauge just how lost I am. She doesn't know what I'm thinking, doesn't know that I feel like I'm in some kind of a strange dream that I can't wake up from, a dream where everything is wrong, including the damn century.

"I didn't mean to be any trouble," I whisper, shaking my head.

Her eyes widen, and she leans back slightly. "You're no trouble at all. I'd just like to know where you're from and a little about you, if you're going to stay here a while."

"Of course." I turn the glass on the table. "I'm from Houston, Texas. My friends and I came out this way on a hunting trip. I don't know where they went off to."

"Well, you can stay here at my place as long as you need to, or at least until your friends show up." She gives me a faint smile that indicates she's not afraid of me, which is good, considering I am a stranger in a time when the west was wild.

I take another drink, letting the warmth of the whiskey burn down my throat. "Thank you, Miss Calloway. I'll help you out around here. Whatever you need, I'll do it."

She raises an eyebrow, her forehead crinkling with skepticism. "You're hurt, but maybe when you're better."

Either way, I need to earn my keep around here, no matter how injured I may be. I also need to understand how this happened. How did I end up in this world, so far from the life I knew? The life I had back home, with Eli, the guys, and with Marissa.

The thought of her hits me hard. I never thought I'd miss her this much, not after the mess she made of things. She cheated on me, and I've told myself over and over that I'm better off without her, but in a place like this, without anything familiar, thinking about her makes it feel like a part of me is missing.

"You're thinking pretty hard over there." Joanna's voice breaks through my thoughts. She smiles, but I can tell she's not sure what I'm wrestling with. She probably doesn't understand what it means to have everything you know ripped away in an instant.

I glance at her, trying to keep my face neutral. "Yeah." I force a chuckle. "Just… wondering where it all went wrong, ya know?"

She nods, like she understands I need time to adjust. "Well, whenever you're ready for more rest, the bed and some supper are in the spare room."

"Thank you." I intend to get up and move back to the bedroom, but my thoughts keep drifting, and I'm frozen in my chair. There's so much I don't know about this place—or this time period. When she moves across the room to start some chores, I excuse myself, thankful for some space to clear my head. She gives me a gentle nod over her shoulder, and I make my way to the spare room. The bed is soft, the room quiet, but sleep doesn't come easily.

I lie in bed staring at the ceiling, the pain, confusion, and impossibilities of the day pressing down on me. There's too much I don't understand, and I have far too many questions without answers. How did I get here? And more importantly, how do I get back home?

If I must stay, I have to make myself useful to Joanna. I can't stay here without pulling my weight. She doesn't owe me anything, and I'm not about to let her take care of me just because I ended up in the wrong damn century.

It's going to take time to get used to this new way of life, with no running water, electricity, phones or even any people that I know, but the one thing I do know is this: I'm not going to just sit around. I'll earn my keep here. I'll prove that I'm not just some drifter who stumbled in.

A WEEK AND A HALF LATER, MY LEG'S HEALING NICELY, THOUGH I STILL have a bit of a limp. Ace is as close as ever, sticking by me like he always does, and we've gotten used to the rhythm of the work, helping Joanna with the cattle and the ranch chores. Joanna's dogs, Huck, Lady, and Margot, are solid herders, and I've come to respect the way Miss Calloway runs her operation.

It's peaceful here, and I've learned a lot about Joanna. She runs this place on her own and employs a few farmhands. She doesn't flinch in the face of hard work, and she doesn't let anyone push her around, not even when the bills pile up.

Joanna and I are fixing a broken wagon wheel when Andy approaches. He's an older man, probably about my dad's age, with a kind smile and a red beard that matches what's left on the sides of his head. "Jake," he calls, wiping his forehead with the back of his hand. "What breed of dog is Ace, anyway? I've never seen a dog quite like him."

I glance down at my best friend. "He's a German Shorthaired

Pointer," I reply. "A bird dog. When he picks up the scent of a bird, he freezes and points. He helps me hunt quail and pheasant."

Andy raises an eyebrow, clearly intrigued. "Bird dog, huh? Never heard of anything like that."

"He's a great hunting partner. He points at the covey until I can get there. Then I kick up the bird, shoot it, and ol' Ace retrieves it."

Joanna looks up from her work, her interest piqued. "A bird dog?" she says. "I'd like to see him in action."

I nod. "He's something special. I'll show you sometime, if you want."

Just as I finish speaking, I hear the unmistakable sound of hooves thudding on the dirt path. I turn to see a tall man on horseback. His clothes are clean and look brand new, but there's something about the way he sits atop his horse, nose in the air, like he already owns whatever he wants that tells me he's no stranger to the others.

Joanna stands a little straighter as he approaches, her lips pursed together like she's holding back a curse word.

The man pulls up beside us, dismounts smoothly, and looks straight at Joanna. "Miss Calloway." His voice is calm but stern. "We need to talk."

He's in Joanna's space like he belongs there, like the swift turn of her shoulders away from him isn't signal enough that he's unwanted. My eyes flicker from her to Andy, who has taken a step back, and then to this clearly unwelcome guest. Who the hell does this guy think he is?

Joanna crosses her arms, her stance firm. "What is it, Mr. Sawyer?"

"You know why I'm here." One side of his mouth pulls up in a tight grin. "You've been avoiding me long enough, but I'm not going to let this go. You can't keep this ranch going alone. You need help."

Joanna's eyes narrow, her chin rising slightly. "I have help!"

He chuckles and glances around, his eyes only slightly hovering on my face before he says, "Not a bunch of ranch hands who know nothing about how to run a business."

I take a step forward, but Joanna stills me with a quick shake of her head. "You don't know what the hell you're talking about, Chase."

As if he wasn't already breathing down her neck, when he takes another step forward, she's cornered against the wagon wheel with nowhere to go. My back straightens, and my hands fist and unfist of their own volition. "You're struggling, Joanna. Everyone knows it. You've got creditors ready to pounce. I'm offering you a deal. Marrying me is the only way you keep all of this—your cattle, the house, and your father's land."

"This is *my* land, Chase! I've worked these cattle with hired help for four years, and I don't need your land, your cattle, or your offer." Her voice doesn't waver. "I can handle this on my own."

Chase's lips twist into a grimace, showing his teeth. "Sure, you've managed for four years. Four years of acquiring nothing but crippling debt. You need a partner, little lady. That's not something these back-woods fellas of yours can provide." He gestures at Andy and then at me, as if he has any idea who I am or what I'm capable of. I take a step forward.

Joanna moves toward him, and Chase backs up, so I freeze. "I've come this far without your help. I'll keep doing it on my own."

Sawyer stares at Joanna for a long moment, his jaw tight, before he finally sighs and turns back to his horse. "You'll change your mind," he mutters. "You'll see that you can't do this without me, Little Miss Stubborn. When I come back, you'd better be ready to get hitched."

Joanna says nothing, and none of us moves until the patter of Sawyer's hoofbeats echoes down the lane. Then, she exhales sharply and wipes her brow on the back of her hand.

I wait a beat before speaking. "Who the hell was that guy?" My hands are still fisted. I slowly relax them, moving toward her. The urge to wrap my arm around her shoulders, to comfort her, is over-whelming, but she doesn't know me well enough, and the last thing she needs is another man intruding into her personal space.

With her lips scrunched to one side of her pretty face, she says, "My neighbor. He's persistent, but I've made myself clear. He's not welcome here. Never has been."

"You sure put him in his place." Pride swells in my chest, and I smile at her. It takes a lot to stand up to someone with the gumption of a man like Sawyer. The way she stood her ground shows strength of character. She's running this ranch on her own, fighting off the people who think she's weak or desperate, and she's not backing down. It's clear that what she's doing here, what she's built, is something worth fighting for.

"I do my best." She takes another deep breath and then turns back to the wheel.

We work in silence, the usual resolve back in her movements. When we're finally finished, she says, "I'm ready for a drink."

I nod, my respect for her growing with each passing moment, but there's something else creeping in, something complicated. I don't know how long I'll be stuck in this time, or how I'll get back to where I came from, but something about Joanna makes me think about Marissa less often now. There's something about how she stands up for herself without making a fuss, how she offers help without needing anything in return. She's incredibly beautiful with those big green eyes and pretty blonde hair, but it's her tenacity that keeps pulling me in. Although I know I'm stuck in a century I don't belong in, she has me thinking maybe it's not so bad after all.

4

OLD-FASHIONED

Andy and I ride through the dry grass, the horses' hooves kicking up dirt with each step. Margot, Huck, and Lady trail behind us, their bodies taut and focused as they move in sync with us, ready to help herd the loose bull. I tighten my fingers on the reins and glance over at Andy. His eyes are narrowed, but his posture is loose in the saddle. He's been at this a lot longer than I have, and his confidence makes me feel a little steadier, even though my stomach is in knots.

"We need to get him back inside of his pen. If he gets in with the herd, we'll be chasing chaos all day." Andy removes his hat and drags a hand through his damp hair.

The bull is already agitated, roaming on the outskirts of the pasture, tossing his head in the air, his muscles rippling with each step. We can't afford to let him get any further. Beasts like him don't give warnings.

The dogs bark in sharp bursts, circling wide to cut off his escape, but it isn't enough. The bull is too smart, too fast, already angling for a gap. I glance back at the dogs, signaling for them to hold. They're doing their best, but keeping control is harder when the bull refuses to settle.

"Stay with me, Joanna!" Andy pulls his horse closer to mine.

We guide our horses toward the bull, trying to turn him back toward the corral. The animal swings his massive head our way, snorting low as he breaks into a charge straight for Chaco.

My heart jumps. "Chaco, move!" I yank the reins, trying to pull him aside, but the bull is already too close.

A sharp whistle cuts through the chaos. The bull falters, hooves digging into the dirt as his attention shifts.

Jake rides hard, shouting and waving his arm, drawing the bull's focus just long enough for it to hesitate.

"Jake!" I shout, fear tightening my chest.

Andy doesn't hesitate. He spurs forward, rope spinning, and sends it clean over the bull's horns. The line snaps tight, jerking the animal's head sideways as it bellows.

I throw my rope on instinct, catching it around the bull's neck. This time, the momentum breaks. The bull stumbles, fighting the pull of both lines.

"Hold him!" Andy calls, his horse bracing as the rope strains.

The dogs rush in, barking sharply now, cutting off escape routes and pressing the bull where we need him to go.

It isn't quick, and it isn't clean, but the pressure holds. Slowly, we force the bull back into the pasture.

When the gate is secured, I finally breathe. My hands tremble as I steady Chaco.

Jake reins up a short distance away, his horse lathered, dust clinging to his sleeves. His chest rises and falls hard, but his eyes are clear.

"That was reckless," I say. "You could've been killed."

Jake meets my eyes. "He was coming straight at you."

Andy lets out a breath, shaking his head. "Smart riding," he says. "You bought us the turn we needed."

I don't like how tight my chest feels when I look at Jake. "Next time," I say, "don't make me watch you try to get yourself killed."

Jake's mouth twitches. "I'll do my best."

Andy laughs under his breath. "That's about as close to a thank-you as you're going to get."

I turn back to Chaco, rubbing his neck until his breathing settles, but I can still feel Jake's presence behind me—steady, unassuming, and far too willing to put himself in harm's way.

With the bull safely back in its rightful pasture, we gather our horses and the dogs, ready to head back to the house. The tension in my shoulders slowly fades, but my heart still races from the adrenaline of the chase.

Despite my lack of saying so, I can't help but be grateful for Jake's help. Albeit, I'm still a little shaken by the risk he took. I haven't known him long. Honestly, I know very little about him at all. Yet, he was willing to risk his life to save mine.

When the day's work is almost done, the cattle are settled along the river, the horses grazing in the lower pastures, and I'm checking over the gear and tools for the night, I feel a sense of accomplishment. But even with everything in its place, my mind won't stop turning over the debts—the taxes and all the other bills I haven't managed to pay. There's always something that needs buying, so the debt and the worry never leave.

Every month the bills pile up higher, and it becomes even more impossible to dig my way out. The property taxes are due in just a few weeks, and I don't know how I'm going to come up with the money this time. I've been fighting tooth and nail to keep the ranch since my folks died a few years back. No matter how hard I work, it always feels like I'm on the edge of losing it all.

Jake's only knowledge of my situation comes from Sawyer's threats, and yet, he's been a big help since he arrived. He's always eager to lend a hand, even with his leg still sore. I don't know how long he plans to stay, but for now, I'm grateful for the extra set of hands.

I push the worry back to the darkest corner of my mind and approach the group of men huddled by the barn.

"Anything else need finishing up?" I ask, walking toward Jake, Andy, Jim, and Ed.

Andy gives me a nod. "All done for today. You ready to head to town? Las Cruces isn't that far."

I glance at Jake, who's gathering up tools. "Andy and me are heading to town to pick up supplies," I tell him. "You can come with us. I think it'll do you good to get off the ranch for a bit."

He looks up at me and nods. "Sounds like a good idea."

We leave the others behind and head toward the wagon. The ride into town is a long one. Jake never quite settles, adjusting his grip when the wheels hit a rut, his attention pulled in every direction. I'm used to the road—and to the worry that comes with it—but I keep my focus forward.

Once we arrive at the supply store, Mr. Isaac Roberts comes over to greet us. "Here for supplies, Joanna?"

"Yes, sir," I say, trying to keep my voice strong. Andy and Jake stand behind me, ready to load up supplies as soon as we're given permission.

The store owner clears his throat and gives me an awkward tight-lipped smile. "Joanna, you still have a fifty dollar balance on your account. You may want to square it up while you're here."

"I'll have it for you soon, Mr. Roberts. I promise."

Mr. Roberts waves a hand, trying for a casual shrug. "Ah, don't worry yourself too much, Joanna. I know things get tight, and we all have our seasons." But the crease between his brows tells me he means the opposite. He's being extra kind, softening the edges for my sake. I've known him since I was a little girl, back when my pa used to bring me here after chores, and I can tell he's worried; not just about the money, but about me.

"Thank you, Mr. Roberts," I say, my tone a little shakier than I'd like. The pressure builds behind my eyes, and I realize suddenly that I could really use a stiff drink.

Jake and Andy help me load bags of flour, coffee, and other necessities. When we're done, I swallow hard, forcing a smile. "Why don't we stop by the saloon?"

"I'm going to stop in and say hello to Doc Jenkins, and I'll meet you there later," Andy says.

I nod and offer Jake my brightest smile. "You've earned a shot of whiskey, and I think we both need it."

"All right." Jake winks. "But only if you're buying."

I laugh. "I think I can swing that." It isn't true. I really shouldn't be spending my hard-earned money on liquor, but I need something to take my mind off my troubles.

As we make our way toward the saloon, I feel the heaviness of the day finally start to lift, if only for a moment. I've fought so hard to keep everything together, but sometimes I have to let go, even if it's just for a little while.

The saloon is full. Men shout, glasses are filled with beer, and the piano player in the corner taps out a lively tune. It smells of whiskey, cigar smoke, and the sharp tang of sweat. A few saloon girls, dressed in bright skirts and bodices that cinch at the waist, move between tables, offering flirtatious smiles as they deliver drinks and accept tips. I lead Jake in, and even amid the noise and ruckus, I can tell he's taking it all in, his eyes moving over the room like he's never been inside a tavern before.

"You sure you're from Houston?" I ask, sliding onto a barstool.

He grins, tilting his head. "That's one thing I am sure of. Why do you ask?"

"Just seems like you've never seen the inside of a saloon before, but I know they have 'em in Texas. Or maybe you're more of a church goin' fella?"

He chuckles and leans closer. "I've been inside a bar before. Just certainly never one quite this… old fashioned."

I raise an eyebrow, smirking. "Oh, so we are old-fashioned? Well, don't let us drag you down, Mr. High Society."

He laughs, and I order us a couple of drinks. The bartender sets two glasses of whiskey in front of us, and Jake lifts his, nodding. "To Las Cruces," he says, "and her old-fashioned ways."

I laugh, clinking my glass lightly against his, and watch him take a sip, his eyes never leaving mine. There's something about the way he just lets things be that comforts me, and for the first time in a long while, I feel like I don't have to pretend. With Jake, I can just be myself, and forget about the pressures of the ranch.

But then, I notice Jake's gaze shift, drawn to the poker table in the corner. A few men are already shouting, slamming chips onto the table in a mix of excitement and frustration.

"Thinking of joining them?" I ask, a little wary.

He shrugs, a grin tugging at his lips. "Might as well see what the fuss is about."

I shake my head, trying not to laugh. "I hope you know what you're getting yourself into."

Jake approaches the table, and I watch, curious, as the men size him up. One of the bigger men scoffs. "You sure you want in, stranger?"

Jake sets the bag he wears on his back down with a thud, then pulls something out and holds it up for the men to see. It's a small, shiny object that glints in the low light of the saloon. His expression is calm as he places it on the table. "I don't have any coin on me," Jake says. "But I'll put this up for the first round, if that's all right."

The men exchange confused looks, clearly unsure of what they're seeing. One of them leans forward, squinting at it. "What kind of contraption is that?" he asks, his voice full of suspicion.

Jake smiles. "It's a new type of wristwatch. I got it in France," he explains. I arch an eyebrow, and he winks at me. I don't think he's ever been to France....

The men glance at each other again, clearly intrigued but still hesitant. One of them says, "It does look European."

I can see the doubt in their eyes, but eventually, the dealer shrugs, as if giving in to curiosity more than anything else. "Well, let's see if you're worth it then," he says, and the game picks up, the tension in the room thicker than before.

Seated across from the dealer, Jake plays it cool, not giving anything away. The men laugh, slap their hands on the table, and trade jabs between rounds, but there's something different about the way Jake plays. His style isn't flashy. There are no big gestures or showmanship. He just plays in calm, quiet moves.

He wins the first hand. No one says anything, but the mood of the room changes. A few of the men exchange glances, but nobody reacts negatively. I shift uncomfortably on my barstool, wondering if I should go get Andy in case there's a brawl.

Jake's face is unreadable, and the others seem unsure of how to respond. They play on, still joking, but the next hand, they're watching him more closely. When Jake wins again, it's a little harder to ignore. The laughter quiets down, replaced by a few muttered comments, though I can't make out what they're saying. The men are suddenly more focused on their cards, their hands tighter, their movements sharper. Jake doesn't smile, doesn't celebrate; he just collects his winnings with a casual ease, like he's used to winning.

The tension builds with every hand. The others start to raise their bets, some of them looking sideways at Jake, trying to figure him out.

Another round, another win for Jake. The coins stack up in front of him, and it's getting harder for the others to hide their frustration. The entire room is quieter now and filled with uncertainty. It's obvious to everyone but Jake that the men think he's cheating. There are no more jokes and no more casual banter. Their faces are tense, their eyes sizing him up.

Just then, Andy enters the saloon and joins me at the bar. He orders a drink from the bartender before looking over at Jake and the poker table.

"Half the room's about ready to string him up," I mutter.

Andy chuckles softly, taking a sip of his drink before setting it down. He glances back at Jake, where the tension is building. "If he's not careful," he says, his tone casual but with an edge of warning, "they're gonna accuse him of cheating. Not many people walk into a game like this and start raking in pot after pot without someone getting suspicious."

I look back at the table, where Jake is stacking coins with a focused calm that only seems to irritate the other players even more. The energy in the room has shifted, and I feel like it might be smart if all three of us headed for the door.

Jake glances over at me, eyes sparkling, and I shake my head, amused, exasperated, and a bit worried. He's only been in town about an hour, and already he's stirred up a hornet's nest.

Even with the annoyance radiating off the other men, I find myself watching him more closely, noting the confidence in his movements, the ease in his composure.

I sip my whiskey, trying to keep my expression even, but it's no use. My lips betray me, pulling into a smile before I can stop them. There's something about Jake Rawlins that keeps me wondering what he'll do next, and no matter how hard I try, I can't seem to look away.

5

GAME OVER

I keep my cards close and force myself to stay nonchalant. I've won more than I should tonight, and the men across the table are accusing me of cheating. The jingle of coins, the shuffle of cards, and the low murmur of whiskey-soaked voices feels familiar, but the comfort is gone.

The man across from me leans back in his chair, jaw tight, eyes glinting under the brim of his hat. Another scratches his chin beneath a scraggily beard, scowling. His finger twitch near the coins. I can feel it—my luck's gone too long. They're pissed. One of them slams his fist on the table, scattering the coins, muttering something about payback.

Then, I see Andy and Joanna coming from the bar. Andy raises his voice just enough to cut through the murmurs. "Hey, let's get out of here. Game's over." Joanna's right beside him. I don't hesitate—this is my chance to leave before things get worse.

"Yeah, I'm out," I say, slipping my winnings into my pocket. This is too much trouble for too little fun.

We weave through the tables, the crowd parting just enough for us to slip through. A drunk guy I cleaned out earlier stumbles after us, mumbling and swaying, the smell of whiskey coming off him in ripe waves. I try to ignore him, let it go, get in the wagon, and leave this saloon behind, but then he makes a huge mistake.

He grabs Joanna with clumsy, rough hands. "If you don't give me my money back, I'm keeping your girl," he slurs, holding her around the waist.

My blood runs cold. He doesn't know me, and that's his mistake. Stepping forward, I tug his hands off her and move her out of the way before swinging my fist once, hard, and the guy crumples to the floor. He's out cold.

Everyone else in the bar goes still. A man in a nice suit near the door throws his hands up. "Not my business," he declares, stepping out of our way.

We make it out into the evening air. The wagon is waiting. Andy climbs onto the bench first, then Joanna slides in, gripping my arm for balance. I push off and jump into the back with the supplies.

The wagon lurches forward, rolling over the rutted street as the saloon shrinks behind us. Coins clatter in my pocket. The players' expressions are burned into my memory, and the futile threat of the drunk idiot is gone, nothing but dust in the night.

Joanna settles beside Andy, shooting me a sideways glance and shaking her head. "You didn't have to—"

I shrug, keeping my eyes on the road ahead. "I didn't have to hit him, but I didn't like the idea of him touching you." My voice is low with a dangerous growl not intended for her.

The wagon bumps along the makeshift road, dirt clouds curling behind us. When we reach Andy's small house, tucked near the edge of Joanna's ranch, I hop down and offer a hand to Joanna, helping her climb down.

Andy swings open the gate and waves us toward the porch. "This is my home, Jake," he says. "And this is my wife."

The pretty redheaded woman in the doorway has curious eyes and a quick smile. She pauses for a heartbeat as she sizes me up.

Andy gestures in my direction. "Kathleen, this is Jake."

"Good evening," she says.

I offer a nod and move forward to shake her hand. "Good evening, ma'am."

"Nice to finally meet you," she says with a friendly smile. "I've heard a lot about you."

"Most of it good, I hope," I joke, and we all chuckle.

"Mostly." She has a twinkle in her eye that tells me she's got a good sense of humor.

Andy tips his hat to Joanna. "I'll see you in the morning." He heads into the house, his wife beside him.

Joanna and I climb back into the wagon, her dogs, Huck, Lady, and Margot, emerging from the shadows, their tails wagging. Ace bolts forward, barking softly as he leaps into the wagon, and I scratch him behind the ears.

We park the wagon in Joanna's barn, guiding the horses to the pasture. Then we head into the house, the dogs following close behind.

Once inside the kitchen, Joanna pours two glasses of water and sets one in front of me. We sit at the table, and she studies me for a moment, then lifts an eyebrow. "So… you caused quite the calamity in town tonight. How much did you win?"

I reach into my pocket and lay the coins on the table, counting them out: ninety-six dollars.

Her eyes fill with awe. "Ninety-six? That's… that's a lot of money."

I can't help but do the quick math in my head. It's probably close to three thousand dollars in my time.

Joanna shakes her head, stunned. "I wouldn't show my face in that saloon again any time soon if I were you."

I shrug, keeping my tone casual. "It's a little more than I expected myself. I hope you don't mind me asking this, Miss Calloway, and feel free to tell me to mind my own business, but how did you end up with this ranch?"

Her expression tightens for a heartbeat, and then she leans back. "My parents died of consumption five years ago." Her voice is quiet but unwavering. "They left it to me. I've been trying to keep up with everything since then. The bills, the livestock, the taxes…."

I let that settle, taking a deep breath. "I can only imagine." Ace nudges my hand, and I pet his head. "It sounds like you've done well, though, keeping things going on your own."

She lets out a short laugh, but I can see the worry lingering in her eyes. "I'm not all alone. I've got Andy and Kathleen, Jim and Constance, and Ed and Laurel. They've got a whole herd of children, and I've got my dogs. But there are days I feel like I'm barely treading water." She glances around the room, her eyes landing briefly on the dogs lying near the hearth, then back at me. "These three help." Huck and Lady are curled up together, and Margot moves to rest at Joanna's feet.

I nod again, careful not to press too hard, but my curiosity and respect are genuine. "It takes courage," I say quietly, "to keep it all running and handle it alone."

Her eyes meet mine, just for a moment. "Courage—or stubbornness." A wry smile breaks through. "Maybe both." She pauses, studying me for a moment, before asking casually, "So, what did you do back in Houston?"

I shift in my seat, my mind briefly racing. I'm honestly surprised she hasn't asked the question before. I should've prepared, just in case. I can't exactly tell her I was an EMT. She wouldn't underhand. Instead, I give her the truth, just not all of it. "I help people," I say simply, trying to keep it vague. "Kind of like a doctor, but in emergency situations. You know, when people need help fast."

"That certainly sounds like a noble thing to do." She smiles at me, leaning against the counter. "You mean you help people when they get knocked out cold in a bar fight?"

We both laugh, and I nod my head. "Not if I'm the one knocking them out."

She asks, "Have you ever gone on a cattle drive?"

"No," I admit. "But I'd like to. It sounds like one hell of an adventure."

"It is. I mean, there are long days, and it's hard work. The dirt, sun, and the cattle will test your patience, but if you're up for it, we're leaving at dawn. You'd better get some rest tonight."

I give a short nod, wondering why I'm just now hearing of this. Perhaps she didn't trust me enough before to invite me along. "I'll be ready."

I head toward the back of the house, Ace at my side. Since all the bunkhouses are full of families, Joanna has given me a room here. Ordinarily, it wouldn't be acceptable for a young woman to have a man like me staying in her house, but everyone here respects Joanna enough not to question the arrangement. Stripping down to the old-fashioned underwear the other fellas loaned me, along with several other mismatched articles of clothing, I get comfortable in bed, thinking about the ride tomorrow. Dawn will come early, and with it, a new challenge. Maybe if I'm lucky, it'll bring a chance to better earn Joanna's trust along the way.

I lie there, staring at the ceiling, trying to make sense of all of this. I don't know how I ended up here or how to get back. Everything from my old life feels like a distant memory, a place I can't reach. Marissa's still in my thoughts, but not nearly as often.

The reality of being stuck in this time is setting in, but I wonder if there's a way back to the future. Then, I think about ending up in this exact place, at this moment in history…. I must be here for a reason. Surely, I'm meant to help the Calloway ranch survive.

It seems like Joanna's business is hanging on the edge of a cliff. I hear it in her tone and in the way she speaks about the bills. I see it in the weariness in her posture when she thinks no one's paying attention. Tomorrow, she's beginning the journey of taking her cattle to market, and I can't help but feel like that's my chance to step in. It'll be a long trip, uncomfortable as hell, and it's the kind of challenge that demands every ounce of grit. If I can prove myself out there, maybe I can help her keep this place going. Maybe I'll find more purpose than just drifting through this strange time. Maybe I'll actually do something that makes a difference.

6

ROPE AND RIDE

Joanna

The sun's just starting to rise, the light spilling across the land stretching out in front of us. The sound of hooves crunching on the dirt trail is usually soothing, but my mind's elsewhere. The fear of losing everything tugs at my every thought. I try not to think about it, but it's there. No matter how many cattle I herd or how many miles I ride, it's always in the back of my head, nagging at me.

But today is meant to be different. Today, we're heading out on the cattle drive. If we can get them to Mesilla, it'll be a solid payday, but I can't shake the fear that even after we sell this herd, it won't be enough. I've been trying to hold it all together for years, but now, I'm not sure how much longer I can keep pretending I have it under control.

My hands are busy guiding Chaco along the narrow trail, but my heart is in my throat. First, we have to round up all the cattle, and then we'll make the eighteen-mile trip southwest to Mesilla. It's a long haul, but we'll make it. I know we will.

The men ride ahead of me: Andy, Ed, Jim, and Jake. I can't help but find myself looking his way more than I should. Every time our eyes meet, I feel a flutter in my chest. Something's happening between us, whether I have the time or the energy for it or not. And damn if I don't keep wondering what's in that bag he wears strapped to his back, like it's full of secrets I'm not supposed to discover.

I watch him as he rides my mare Bridgit, his dog, Ace, trotting alongside. That smart ol' dog's getting the hang of it, just like Jake is. Ace is picking up the commands, watching the cattle with the same level of attention as the rest of us.

I can't help but admire how well Jake fits in, even though he said he's never been on a cattle drive before. He doesn't make a fuss and doesn't ask too many questions. He just rides, works, and every so often, breaks into that damn song about being a cowboy.

He's been singing loudly enough that the rest of us can hear it off and on for the past hour. Something about how he should've learned to rope, ride, and wear a six shooter. There's a verse about a Miss Kitty, and every time he gets to that part, Ed snickers, Andy sings along, and even Jim cracks a smile. At first I bit my lip, but I couldn't help but chuckle, too. It's ridiculous, and yet, there's something endearing about it.

"Well, you've got the singing part down," Ed calls, a big grin on his haggard face. "Next thing we know, you'll be wrangling cattle with your voice alone."

Jake just shrugs, his lips curling into that debonair smile of his. "It's all part of my charm." He winks at me, and a surge of heat fans through me.

I shake my head, trying to hide the smile that's pulling at my lips.

We have the first group of cattle, and they are moving along nicely as we move to the next pasture to gather more. Chaco's steady gait matches the slow pace of the herd, and all is relatively quiet. A sharp crack splits the air, and I jerk my head up, instinctively pulling Chaco's reins tight. I scan the horizon. From behind a cluster of rocks, a group of men on horseback emerges, rifles in hand. They're wearing handkerchiefs over their faces.

Another shot rings out, this one close enough to send the cattle in all directions, their nerves spiking. I tighten my hands on the reins, and my heart pounds. The bastards are here to try to steal my cattle.

I don't hesitate. I let out a sharp whistle, and Margot launches forward, her powerful body cutting through the dust. One of the riders barely has time to react before she's on him, her jaws clamping down on his boot and calf. He yells as she yanks hard, dragging him clean out of the saddle.

He hits the ground with a brutal thud, the breath knocked from his lungs. Margot's on top of him instantly, her teeth snapping, keeping him pinned as he scrambles and curses in the dirt.

The other men shout, startled by the sudden violence. Huck and Lady surge in next, darting at the horses' legs and snapping at dangling boots. One rider nearly loses his seat as Lady lunges, forcing his horse sideways. Another fires wildly, the shot going wide as Huck snaps at his stirrup.

Before I can draw another breath, Jake rides hard into my line of sight, angling his horse between me and the gunfire. His hand drops to his holster—then stops. I see the hesitation flicker across his face as another shot cracks the air, the bullet tearing past us instead of finding its mark.

"Don't waste your bullets!" I shout to my fellas. "The dogs are pushing them off!"

Ace barrels in alongside my dogs, barking and snapping, adding to the chaos. The horses rear and spin, panic rippling through the group. One of the men curses loudly, hauling on his reins as they break formation.

Within seconds, the would-be thieves are retreating, wheeling their horses hard and riding off in a cloud of dust, shots fired blindly behind them as warning rather than aim.

Margot remains with the fallen man, standing over him, her chest heaving, teeth bared. He isn't getting up.

The dust settles slowly. The cattle mill, shaken but intact.

I keep my grip on the reins tight, my pulse hammering. "That's far enough," I mutter. "They won't be back today."

The chaos dies down quickly. Margot's still standing over the man she attacked, her jaws dripping with blood, and Huck and Lady come over to investigate. Sweat, blood, and a suffocating amount of dust fill the air.

Adrenaline pumps through my veins, but I keep a tight hold on the reins. Chaco's unwavering obedience helps to calm the nerves that are trying to jump out of me. I glance at the fallen attacker, feeling my blood boil. These men tried to steal from me, tried to kill us, and now one of them is lying unmoving in the dirt. I don't feel a bit sorry for him, but the gravity of the situation hits me hard.

Jake rides up beside me, his gun drawn, scanning the ridges and tree lines. When he looks at me, he doesn't say anything, but I can see the question in his eyes. *Are you all right?*

I nod, though I'm not sure if I am. "They won't be attacking anyone us again soon," I say, but my voice feels too tight, too harsh, even for me. I swallow—hard—and try to push it down. There's no time for weakness now.

"Let's get the cattle rounded back up and moving," I call out, trying to control my tone. I'm already focused on the herd and the long miles ahead. The dogs fall back into their positions, and the men get back to work. It's the only thing we can do now. These bastards don't even deserve a shallow grave.

Jake looks into my eyes once more, and then looks away just as quickly, like he's trying not to be too obvious about his concern. I don't need it. Not right now. I just need to get these cattle to Mesilla— and to survive another day.

I force myself to concentrate on the herd again. We're far from done, and there's no turning back now.

* * *

THE SUN'S SINKING LOW BEHIND THE DISTANT HILLS. THE NIGHT AIR IS cooler but still carries the lingering heat from the brutally hot day. I strike flint against steel, and sparks catch the dry brush until the fire takes hold and dances in the growing darkness. The scent of burning wood fills the air, mixing with the earthy undertones of the river where we just washed the grime off the dogs.

The Rio Grande isn't far from the trail, but the water is cold enough to make my skin tighten and gooseflesh rise. I'm still reeling from the insanity of what happened this afternoon. The sound of the gunfire, and the sight of that man's body sprawled on the ground—it all happened so fast, and even though it's over, I can't shake the tension that still flows through my veins.

The animals are restless, their senses sharp after the chaos of the afternoon. I keep glancing over at the horses and the cattle, making sure they're settled, but they all seem to be on edge.

Jake moves toward me with his strange canteen in his hand. There's something odd about the way he holds it, like he's got a trick up his sleeve.

"Here," he says, holding out a small, flat tablet in his hand. "Drop this in your canteen," he says, dropping a tablet into his own.

"What's that?" I ask, my voice low, trying not to sound too suspicious.

"It cleans the water," Jake replies, his eyes catching mine. "It makes the river water safe to drink. You don't want to get sick out here."

I look up at him, thrown off a little. I've never heard of such a thing. I don't trust it, but for some reason, I trust him. "You drink yours first," I say, still slightly skeptical.

He shrugs and chugs his water. "It works just fine. You'll see. Trust me, Miss Calloway. I'm not as strange as I look."

I can't help but laugh, and it feels good to forget about the day's troubles for a moment. I try the water, and though it tastes a little different, that's the only change I notice.

We set up camp properly, gathering the gear, making sure the fire's strong. Jim and Andy set their bedrolls a few yards from the fire, and Ed is already pulling out the tin plates for dinner. The usual evening routine is falling into place, but it feels different tonight. The air is filled with unsaid words, with the intensity of everything that happened earlier.

We sit around the fire, dinner cooked and served in silence, the only sounds the crackling of the flames and the occasional soft snort from the horses. The food is simple—beans and beef. I eat slowly, trying not to let my thoughts wander too far.

Then Jake breaks the quiet. "Why didn't you want us shooting at those assholes?"

His question catches me off guard, and I hesitate before answering. "I didn't want their blood on our hands," I say finally, my voice firm. "The dogs had the situation handled. There was no need for us to get involved any more than we already were."

Jake's gaze softens, his mouth twitching into that smile that's too damn distracting. "You're something else, Miss Calloway," he says, and the hint of admiration in his voice is hard to miss. I can't help but feel warmth and pride deep in my chest.

Jim, Andy, and Ed finish their meal, too tired for conversation. The two older fellas retire to their bedrolls while Ed goes out to take the first shift of patrolling the herd, leaving just Jake and me by the fire. The night feels colder now, but the warmth between us doesn't fade. I can't help but notice the way the firelight flickers across his face, the shadows playing on the hard planes of his jaw, his lips, and how his green eyes sparkle when he looks at me.

"You sure you're all right?" he asks, his voice softer now, like he's trying to break through the hard shell I've wrapped around myself.

I nod, even though I'm not sure I am. "Yeah. Just... thinking."

He shifts closer, his knee brushing mine, closing the space between us. His eyes dart down to where our legs are touching before looking back up at me.

"I try not to do too much of that if I can help it." His tone is low and teasing.

"I saw you back there," I say. "You got between me and those bullets."

Jake tilts his head slightly, like he's considering my words. A smile tugs at the corner of his mouth. "Of course. I did as any gentleman would."

The words hang between us, and I find myself staring at him a little too long. That familiar flutter fills my chest. For a second, I think he might kiss me. I wait, but he doesn't move closer. He just sits there, looking at me with that damn fetching grin of his.

I shake my head, trying to cover the way my pulse has picked up. "I didn't realize you *were* a *gentleman*."

He keeps smiling, boyish and mischievous, and his eyes never leave mine. "You just wait, Joanna. I'm full of surprises."

7

BLOOD IN THE WATER

JAKE

The morning light creeps across the trail, breaking through the chill of dawn and warming the land. The cattle are already moving, the rhythm of hooves beating hard on the ground as they follow the lead. Jim, Ed, and I are up front, keeping an eye on things while Andy and Joanna ride at the back. I keep thinking about her, remembering the way she looked at me last night. There was definitely something there. I almost kissed her, but I held back, not wanting to move too fast. It's hard to forget that moment, even if it was only a second.

My attention shifts to Ace. He trots alongside us, his ears perked. Watching him fight off those outlaws yesterday, the way he defended us, I couldn't help but feel proud. He's not just a dog. He's a damn good partner.

I glance over at Ed and Jim. Both of them are quiet, just letting the horses and cattle do the work. I figure it's as good a time as any to make small talk rather than continuing to teach them Toby Keith songs. Plus, I'd like to know the men I'm working with.

"So, you fellas live on the Calloway ranch, too?" My eyes drift between them.

Jim looks over at me with a slight smile. "Yes, sir. Close enough to the main house to help Joanna out when needed, but far enough away to have our own space. You'll probably be seeing a lot of us if you stick around."

I nod, trying to make sense of the dynamics. "Y'all have families, then? Wives and kids?"

Jim gives a soft chuckle. "Constance and I have six kids. She keeps the house running, and she's always busy. The oldest is ten. The youngest is only two. Can't say it's ever quiet."

"Six kids?" I raise an eyebrow, impressed. "That's a full house."

"Gets crowded and crazy," Jim says, his tone light. "But it's a good kind of chaos. And Constance, well, she's the one who holds it all together."

"What about you, Ed? You got a family?"

He grins, looking ahead at the herd as he shifts in his saddle. "Yeah, Laurel and I have three little ones. The youngest is barely a three weeks old, and the two boys are already making trouble. That's how it is. Can't keep 'em still for long, but Laurel's good at keeping everything under control. She's a hell of a woman."

"All of that must keep you busy." Clearly, their lives are more than just herding cattle.

"Busier than I'd like sometimes, but I wouldn't trade it," Ed says, his smile widening. "Family's everything."

I think about what it must be like to have someone waiting for you at the end of the day. The thought haunts me, but I keep it to myself. "Sounds like you both got your hands full. You have my utmost respect."

I look back at the cattle and spot Andy and Joanna at the back of the herd, just behind the slower-moving animals. I can't help but wonder how she's holding up, but I don't stare at her too long.

"Any advice for me?" I ask, more for the sake of conversation than anything else. "I'm not exactly a romancer."

Jim gives me a look, his eyes narrowing just a bit. "You mean you have eyes for Joanna?"

"Was it that obvious?" I ask. "How did you know I wasn't speaking in generalities?"

The two cowboys share a knowing laugh, neither of them venturing to answer my questions, and we ride on. The sun's climbing higher now, casting its heat across the land. The cattle are moving at a steady pace, and everything feels calm for the moment. Silence stretches between us, but it's comfortable, the hum of hooves and the occasional call to the dogs filling the air. It's easy to slip into a rhythm when everything's going right, but I can feel the memory of yesterday still pressing down on us.

When we reach a river crossing, the men pull their horses back, guiding the cattle toward the water. The river's running high, and it seems as though the cattle are nervous.

I watch the cowboys move the cattle across the water, studying their moves in case I need to help. A shout from up ahead hits my ears.

"Whoa! Watch out!" Ed shouts.

I snap my head up just as Jim's horse slips on the slick rocks by the riverbank. He's thrown from the saddle, and his leg makes contact with a sharp boulder. A grunt of pain escapes the man's lips as he reaches down toward his injured leg. The water around him is already turning pink.

I don't hesitate. My feet hit the ground, and I'm running toward Jim, my mind racing through the possibilities. I've seen too many injuries in my past, and too many moments like this.

I drop to his side, and immediately see that the gash is bad. His leg's twisted. He landed hard on that rock. Blood pours out fast, soaking through his pants. His face is pale, and he's already sweating from the shock.

"Jim, stay with me," I say. "You're gonna be all right. Don't pass out on me."

He grits his teeth, trying to stay conscious. I can see the pain in his eyes, but he's holding on.

I drag him up onto the shore, which is thankfully only a few feet away, and then reach into my pack, pulling out a tourniquet. I tie it above the wound, tightening it until the blood flow slows down. The pressure on the artery is enough to keep him alive until I can stop the bleeding for good.

"Stay awake, Jim," I say. I know what I'm doing, and I'm not letting him die here.

Ed, Joanna, and Andy stand back, stunned into silence. They don't know what to make of what I'm doing, but I'm not here to explain myself. I just need to get Jim stable.

I clean the wound with antiseptic from my first aid kit and rip open a packet of Hemostatic gauze and press it into the wound, watching as the blood slows even more. His breathing's still shallow, but he's holding on. That's all that matters for now.

"I've got it," I tell him, my voice calm. "You'll be all right."

Jim's leg is badly injured, but for now, he's stable enough. Ed quickly moves to check Jim's mare, running his hands over her sides and feeling for any sign of injury. "She's fine," he mutters, giving the horse a reassuring pat.

Joanna dismounts and steps up to my side, her eyes scanning my patient's pale face. "Jim, you're tough. You've survived far worse than this, buddy," she says, her voice tight with concern. I glance up at her, offering a nod.

"Jim, we're gonna get you back on your feet," I say, trying to keep my voice calm. "You're gonna be fine."

He manages a weak nod, sweat still beading on his forehead. "Yeah... just help me up."

Ed, Andy, and I slowly pull him upright. He winces when he puts weights on his injured leg, but with some effort, we get him back into the saddle. It's not pretty, but he's resilient.

"Thanks, Jake," Jim grits out, his teeth clenched.

I nod. "Just glad I had what I needed to mend that wound."

With Jim back on his horse, we urge the cattle forward, the herd moving across the water. The dogs dart ahead, guiding the slower animals through the shallows. Ace stays close by me, keeping a sharp eye out. The cattle continue to cross, their hooves splashing through the water, and we follow behind, making sure everyone gets through safely.

I turn and watch Joanna bring up the back end of the herd. She doesn't rush or push them, just moves through the water, ignoring the noise, keeping her cows in line. I realize, with a little bit of a sting, that Marissa could never have done anything like this. She wouldn't have lasted five minutes in this kind of heat, with this kind of danger and pressure. But Joanna? She's different. She's so strong and always sure of herself. I've known it from the start, but today, it's hard not to notice just how damn beautiful she is.

"All right, let's get the rest of these animals across," she calls, her voice clear and authoritative.

I fall in line with the others as we make our way across the river, the cold water splashing against our horses' legs. The current is strong, but we keep the cattle moving forward. Jim struggles on his horse a little, but he's managing, his leg not as bad as it could've been. If he would've broken it out here, I can't imagine how I would've helped him. I might not have been able to save him.

I help guide the herd, making sure no one gets stuck in the deeper parts of the river. When we reach the far side, most of us dismount to check that the cattle are safe and the dogs are accounted for. Jim stays in the saddle until Ed can go over to help him down.

"We'll set up here for the night. Jim's hurt, and he needs to rest," Joanna says.

She directs Andy and Ed as they tend to the animals and get a fire started.

I approach Jim where he's sitting on the ground near where the other two cowboys are building the fire. "You good?" I ask, handing him a canteen.

"I just need a minute," Jim replies, his voice rough. "It's damn painful, but I'll manage." He takes the canteen gratefully, then winces as he hands it back to me.

"You need anything else? Whiskey? Food?" I watch him closely.

He nods. "Whiskey'll help. Thank you kindly."

Ed comes over and squats next to us. "He's a tough one, Jake. He'll be fine."

"Yeah," I mutter, my eyes on Jim. "But he's not getting back on his feet tonight." I pull out a flask and hand it to Jim, who drinks it down quickly.

An hour or so later, the fire crackles, smoke rising in the warm afternoon air. We sit around, enjoying the relative quiet. The cattle rest nearby, and the dogs are sprawled out, panting from a long day in the hot sun. Joanna, Andy, and Ed are busy cooking, the smell of meat and onions filling the air. Jim leans his back against a tree, his leg elevated on a log I found. I left my flask with him. Every time he takes a sip of whiskey, he grimaces.

I'm trying not to think about how different this life is from what I'm used to, but it's hard not to notice. The way these people live, the way they work—it's all so strange compared to what I know. I'm used to being around staunch EMTs and firefighters, but these people? They're something else. There's no boasting, no need for recognition, just a kind of strength and courage that makes everything I've known feel small in comparison, despite the fact that I've worked with heroes for years.

After a while, Ed looks over at me, curiosity in his eyes. "So, Jake, where'd you get all that stuff in your pack? I've never seen anything like it. You weren't kidding when you said you could handle yourself."

I hesitate. I've been doing my best to avoid questions like that, but it's too late now. They're all looking at me, waiting for an answer.

"I, uh... got it in Houston," I say, keeping my tone casual. "A little shop down there. Good place to get things that might come in handy if someone gets hurt." It's a weak explanation, but it'll have to do.

Joanna looks at me for a moment, raising an eyebrow. "You really knew what you were doing back there. How did you learn to stop the bleeding like that?"

I swallow hard. I don't have a good answer. I'm not sure what to say. I can't exactly tell her I was trained to do so over a hundred years in the future.

"Just a little training from the doctor in the big city," I say. "Some stuff I picked up over the years."

Joanna's gaze softens a little, but I can tell she's not quite satisfied with my answer. She seems to want to push, to ask more questions, but she doesn't.

"You don't have to explain, Jake," she says after a beat. "I just thought it was impressive, that's all. You helped Jim when no one else could."

I glance over at Jim, who's now resting more comfortably, the whiskey starting to dull the pain. "I just did what I could," I say, shrugging it off. "It's nothing special."

But inside, I know it's something more. I'm keeping a lot of things hidden. There are so many things I can't talk about. I wish I could explain, wish I could tell them who I really am and where I'm really from. But they'd think I lost my mind.

There's a long silence, the crackle of the fire the only sound filling the space between us. I stare into the flames, willing myself not to say anything else, not to give myself away.

Finally, Jim grunts from where he's leaning. "Hell, I'm just glad you were around, Jake. Would've been a lot worse without you."

"Happy to help," I mutter, forcing a smile. "But I'm sure you'll be back on your feet in no time."

"Maybe," he says with a dry laugh. "But tonight, I'm staying put."

Ed hands me a plate of food to take over to Jim, and as I carry it, my thoughts return to the enormous differences between my time and theirs. If this was 2025, we'd just call someone to come and get poor Jim and take him to the nearest emergency room. But not here in 1875. Here, he'll suffer along the trail until we make it home days from now.

And the thought that nags me even more is that Joanna has no idea who I really am, and I don't know how long I can keep pretending to be someone who belongs here.

I wonder if Eli, Logan, Tate, and Ryan are looking for me. I don't even know if getting back is possible, but the longer I stay, the harder it gets to imagine leaving. Joanna makes it worse in a way I try desperately not to admit. I just hope my charade holds together long enough for me to figure out what the hell to do next.

8

MARGOT

Night drapes over the camp, thick and hot. The fire glows low, and smoke burns the inside of my nostrils. The horses shift and snort, chewing and stamping, and the men sit close by, chatting quietly to one another. Otherwise, the night is quiet, except for the soft scrape of hooves, and the rush of the nearby river.

Huck and Lady lie together near the herd, and Ace rests by Jake, quiet and still. Margot curls up beside me, her head on her paws. Andy and Ed laugh about something I didn't catch, and Jim lies on his bedroll nearby. His injured leg is propped up, his rifle resting within reach.

The cattle erupt in nervous lowing, hooves scraping and thudding all around. The dogs lift their heads, and Margot growls. I jump up, grab my rifle, and strain my eyes past the fire. A dark shape darts between two steers, too small and quick to be a cow.

"Wolves," Andy says, loud and clear.

All four dogs explode into motion, barking and tearing through the dark as cattle surge inward, pressing together in panic. More gray shapes slip in, snapping at legs and driving fear deeper into the herd.

Andy fires, the crack of his rifle splitting the air, muzzle flash lighting up a tangle of bodies for half a second.

My heart hammers as I fire at the wolves, one after another. Sweat coats my rifle, making it slick. Shadows twist and dodge between the cattle, fast and unpredictable. I watch a small calf get dragged down by two large beasts and squeeze off another round, then another, every shot ripping through the darkness, frightening the cattle but doing little to send the wolves running.

Then, I hear Margot yelp. She's near the edge of the herd, locked with a wolf that's much bigger than her. The alpha wolf drives Margot sideways as she snaps and twists, trying to stay upright.

Before I catch my breath, Jake is already running toward her. He crosses the distance faster than I think possible, moving between Margot and the wolf. He fires just as the alpha lunges at him. The shot cracks through the night, and the wolf collapses before it can reach her again. He moves to shield her from the other wolves still circling in the darkness.

When their alpha goes down, the rest of the pack scatters or falls under gunfire. Huck, Lady and Ace chase the pack until they're called back. The cattle shift and snort, tense even as the danger passes, gradually easing into the space around them as the fight ends. A few have roamed away. We'll need to bring them back to the herd, but my eyes are on my dog.

Jake kneels in the dirt, his hands pressed into Margot's side. Blood darkens her fur and soaks into his shirt as he talks to her quietly.

I move closer, my heart still hammering, and kneel beside them. Margot's eyes flick toward me, and she gives a weak thump of her tail. I swallow hard.

"She's hurt badly," I say.

"Go grab my bag," he replies.

My hands shake as I run toward the campfire, grab the bag, and hurry back. He opens it and starts pulling out items I only recognize from when he was helping Jim. He grabs small, shiny tools, bright cloth, and a thin, glinting thread unlike anything I've seen.

"What's that?" I ask, pointing to the thread.

"It's called a suture kit," he says, focusing on his work. He threads a large needle with the thread.

"Suture kit?" I echo, squinting. "You're going to sew her up with it?"

"Yes ma'am. It's strong and holds better than regular thread. It's also sterile"

I watch his hands in awe. He talks to Margot the whole time, keeping her calm while I stroke her head and murmur nonsense, promises I don't know how to keep. She's been with me since she was a puppy. She's my best friend, and losing her would rip something out of me I could never replace.

Jake pours something over the deep gash on her side, and Margot whines in pain. I flinch harder than she does.

"I know," he says mostly to her, but also to me. "I know. I've gotta clean it before I can sew it up."

He sews the wound up quickly, and I don't understand how he knows what he's doing, but the bleeding slows.

"She's a tough little gal." He meets my gaze with a reassuring smile. Carefully, the two of us move her back toward the campfire, and she lies down next to me, keeping her head propped on my knee.

I never leave Margot's side, and neither does Jake. I pet her head gently while Jake finishes tending to her wounds, looking her over for any others. When he finds a few smaller, more shallow cuts, he pours medicine from his bottle again.

Time stretches on. The fire burns low until Andy—or maybe Ed—tends to it, feeding the flames back to life. They check on the cattle, the horses, and the other three dogs. Andy brings us water and gives us the news: we lost only a few cattle, the horses held their own, and Huck, Lady, and Ace have only minor wounds and scratches.

"What is that you poured on her wounds?" I whisper later, when Margot is asleep.

"It's called antiseptic. They have it in the city. Keeps the rot out."

I nod, not sure what to think about that. It seems that the big city of Houston has a lot of secrets that might come in handy out here.

Exhaustion settles in, and I finally sit back on the dirt, relaxing a little. I glance at Jake, my throat tight. "Thank you for what you did for Jim earlier and for Margot, too. We wouldn't have made it through today without you, and I don't know what I would do without my best girl. You saved her life. How can I ever repay you?"

"You don't have to thank me, and you certainly don't have to repay me. You took me in when I was hurt and nursed me back to health, Joanna. And Margot is tough. Don't worry. She's going to make it." His smile is confident enough to make me believe it.

Margot's breathing is stronger now. She moves a little, presses her nose into my palm, and lets out a tired sigh. I bend forward and rest my forehead against her face, closing my eyes for just a moment.

* * *

I WAKE WITH MY CHEEK PRESSED INTO THE DIRT AND MARGOT'S FUR beneath my hand. For a second, everything is slow to come into focus. Then, I feel the steady rise and fall of her breath beneath my palm, and sit up, careful not to disturb her.

Jake's already awake, crouched beside her, his sleeves rolled up, his shirt a little damp from the morning heat. He's checking her wound again, his touch gentle, searching for any sign of trouble. In his other hand, he has something small wrapped in paper, which he breaks apart and offers to Margot in pieces.

"What is that?" I ask softly, my voice rough.

"It's a little bit of liver. Ace loves it. I'm sure it smells worse than it tastes. She seems to like it."

Of course, he has treats for his dog, and they came out of that endless pack of his, the one that keeps producing items I've never seen or even heard of until I met Jake. Oh, I've heard of liver, but this bit is small and dried. I never would've thought to give it to a dog as a treat.

Margot eats slowly and carefully. Jake finishes feeding her and sits back on his heels. "She held on through the night." He looks into my eyes. "She'll recover."

I nod. "Thank you again. I am so grateful you're here."

"I'm happy to be here." He looks into my eyes, and all I can think about is kissing his handsome face.

I quickly look away, trying to push the thought out of my mind. I can't—won't—let myself get caught up in that. Not now, not when I need to focus on the herd and my injured companions. I take a deep breath, fighting the blush that creeps up my cheeks. I'm not about to make life more complicated than it already is.

As the camp stirs, and the sky lightens, I watch Jake moving around, checking on the other dogs, offering them treats too. I think about last night, the way he put himself between Margot and that wolf without hesitation.

Bravery is often tied to intense, dramatic moments, but Jake isn't like that. He doesn't seek recognition or a chance to prove himself. He just steps in when it matters most and does what needs to be done.

Problems spin through my mind–as usual. How can I rig something to keep Margot from being jostled? Or should we just slow the herd again? Before I say a word, Jake leads his horse over.

"I'll take her," he says simply.

I arch an eyebrow but don't argue. I have to trust he knows what he's doing.

He lifts Margot carefully, like she weighs nothing at all, and lays her across the front of his saddle. Then he swings up behind her, one hand braced around her body, the other on the reins. Bridgit, my old mare, flicks an ear but stays calm, like she understands exactly what's being asked of her.

"I won't let her fall," he adds, meeting my eyes now. "I promise."

Watching him with Margot, so careful and kind, makes me feel something I've never felt for a man before. I admire him more than I want to admit.

We move out, the herd slow but cooperative, the morning sun already burning hot. Jake cradles Margot all day, adjusting when she shifts, talking to her quietly. He never complains and never asks to trade off. He just takes care of her.

I catch myself looking at him too often, and I know I'm in trouble. This isn't just gratitude anymore. It's the realization that I trust him with my herd, with my people, and with the dog I love most in the world. I'm terrified to admit it, but Jake's the kind of man I could trust with my heart, and I never thought I'd feel that way about anyone.

I've always relied on myself. I've never been interested in partnering with a man, but watching him with Margot, seeing the kindness he gives without expecting anything in return, makes me feel a pull toward him. Something about him makes me think maybe I don't have to be alone anymore.

9

STUBBORN OL' BULL

When we finally reach Mesilla, the market is packed with the noise of people, livestock, and wagons layered over one another until it all blends into a constant hum. Buyers move along the fences, stopping to inspect the cattle. Deals are made. Money is exchanged.

Joanna handles the business herself. She leaves us near the edge of the pens while she speaks with the buyers, listening more than she talks. I can't hear the details, but I can tell when the conversation turns in her favor by the way her face lights up, and the men adjust their posture. Whatever she said, it worked.

I keep an eye on Margot while I wait. She's still sore, but she'll be all right in a day or two. The other dogs stay close by.

When the deal is finished, Joanna gathers everyone together and pays Andy, Ed, and Jim. She counts carefully, making sure each of them gets what they're owed. Andy grins and thanks her. Ed nods and tucks the money away. Jim accepts his share without comment, limping along, mindful of his injured leg.

Then, Joanna turns to me, offering me my cut like it's the most natural thing in the world.

"I can't accept that," I say.

"What do you mean? You worked the drive." She tips her head to the side and studies my face.

"I helped," I say. "But you have offered me your home, food, and hospitality. If anything, I still owe you. We're even at best."

She studies me for a long moment, clearly weighing whether this is an argument worth having. "You're a stubborn ol' bull, Mr. Rawlins." She shakes her head.

I can't help but chuckle. "So I've been told."

"This money is yours." Joanna extends it to me again.

With a shrug, I say, "Keep it."

Her mouth tightens, but she doesn't push further. She stabs the money into her pocket with deliberation and gives me a look that promises this isn't settled in her mind. I let it go for now.

We leave the market and head into town to drop off the dogs with Joanna's friend Shelby while the rest of us spend the evening in town. She lives in a small house not far from the center of Mesilla.

Shelby, a sturdy woman with dark hair graying around the edges, greets us warmly. "What happened here?" She carefully examines the bandages wound around Margot's middle.

"It was a wolf. She'll heal," Joanna says. "I appreciate you looking after them tonight, Shelby."

"Of course." The woman gives me a sharp look. "Just don't do anything you'll regret." Then, she chuckles, and I can't tell if she's teasing or not.

Joanna crouches beside Margot, and the dog leans into her hand before limping inside. Huck, Lady, and Ace follow without protest, already getting comfortable like they understand this is temporary.

Standing, she wipes a tear away from her cheek before turning away. She doesn't say anything more, but I can tell leaving Margot in her current condition hurts her more than she lets on.

We tie Bridgit and Chaco up near the water trough and make sure they have fresh grain before walking farther into the city.

Mesilla is alive with movement, people filling the streets, vendors calling out from their carts, music drifting from nearby taverns.

Joanna walks beside me, and I watch her pretty face as she shifts her attention from one storefront to the next.

"We should probably avoid the bar so you don't make any more enemies," she says with a grin.

I feign exasperation. "If you insist."

We stop at a stall filled with fruit, and Joanna buys us each a peach. Next, we visit a store with bolts of cloth. Joanna runs her fingers over a piece of light blue cloth thoughtfully before setting it back.

"Don't like the color?" I ask her.

She shrugs. "I need to think about it."

I want to buy it for her, thinking maybe it's just too expensive, but I'm not sure if she really doesn't like it or if it's the price tag, so I let it be.

We eat at a small cafe in the heart of the city. The food is delicious and filling. We both scarf down the meal like we haven't eaten in days, savoring each bite. The warm, crusty bread is perfect with the rich, savory stew, and the salad is so fresh it tastes like the vegetables were picked that morning. The meal is simple, but it hits the spot. The cozy atmosphere of the cafe, with its rustic charm and the hum of quiet conversation, makes it feel like we've stumbled upon a hidden gem. For a moment, it's just the two of us, lost in the comfort of our food and one another's company.

Now might be the perfect time to see if Joanna is beginning to feel the same way about me as I am her, but I don't want to do anything to ruin the moment, so I simply savor her presence.

After dinner, we walk down the street. The sun sinks low on the horizon. Joanna's eyes sweep the taverns, scanning with purpose. I follow close, letting her lead. Then she stops and nods slightly toward a line of horses tied outside a bar.

"They must be in here," she says.

I look where she's pointing and see Andy, Ed, and Jim's horses.

Inside, the saloon is lively. Voices carry over fiddle music, and some men are playing cards while others flirt with saloon girls. Our friends are easy to spot, sitting at a table with beer mugs in front of them.

Joanna leads the way over to the table and slides onto the chair beside Jim. I pull up a chair next to her, and she waves to a waitress. "Next round's on me," she says.

Across the room, a poker game is underway, coins stacked up high. When Joanna sees me watching them, she nudges my side.

"Please don't join that game," she whispers.

I raise an eyebrow. "Why not?"

"You'll win again, and they'll hunt us down and gut us." She shakes her head, and I can't tell if she's completely serious or not.

I glance at the table again. Winning would be easy enough, but that doesn't matter tonight as much as keeping Joanna happy does. I can't stop looking at her. Emerald green orbs sparkle in the firelight. Perfect pink lips pucker in slight irritation. Even after days on the trail, her blonde locks gleam from the bun wound on top of her head. Gorgeous doesn't even begin to describe her.

"I'm not playing tonight." I give her a reassuring nod.

The waitress sets our drinks on the table. She takes a sip of her beer and beams. "Good. I appreciate that."

We stay a while, finishing our drinks, and I realize I'm looking at her more than anything else in the room. Eventually, I muster the courage to ask. "Would you like to get some fresh air?"

She nods. "Yes, that sounds nice."

Outside, the street is quieter now, the noise of the saloon reduced to a dull buzz behind the swinging door. Moonlight illuminates her porcelain skin and makes her eyes sparkle.

"The more I get to know you, the more you surprise me." Her voice is soft, barely a whisper.

"Is that a good or a bad thing?" I raise an eyebrow.

With a chuckle, she moves close enough that I can feel the heat from her arm through my sleeve. "It's a very good thing."

I put my hand on her back and pull her close. She grabs my shirt, and our lips finally meet. I hold my breath, savoring the taste of her. I've been wanting to kiss her since the moment we first met.

Realization sets in, and I step back just enough to meet her eyes.

She tilts her head, a teasing glint there. "Would you like to do something fun?" she asks.

"Lead the way." I gesture with one arm, wondering what she has up her sleeve.

At the river's edge, a small rowboat rocks gently against the shore. It's worn smooth, but it seems sturdy. She looks up at me, a spark of mischief in her eyes. "Ever been on the Rio Grande at night?"

"Can't say that I have," I reply. I offer my hand so she can step in first.

It seems it doesn't matter what we're doing. We could be sitting in a tavern, on a boat, or mending a wagon wheel, and everything's just better with her. She makes life feel like it's worth living, like the whole damn world's a little more alive when she's around.

I step into the boat after her. "Whose canoe are we stealing?"

She laughs, covering her mouth. "We're not stealing anyone's canoe. These are just here in case someone needs them."

"Sure, Miss Calloway. I believe you. You've never steered me wrong before." I wink, and that glorious giggle of hers fills the air again. "Get it? Steered?"

"I definitely got it." She shakes her head, the look on her face telling me she thinks I'm ridiculous. Maybe I am.

I laugh at my own joke, take the oars, and push us from the shore. The boat glides smoothly into the current. City noises fade behind us, leaving only the gentle slap of water against the hull and the faint rustle of reeds along the bank.

Joanna looks out across the river, her arms crossed loosely around her knees, and I can't stop staring at her. Her top is a little rumpled, clinging to her curves in a way that makes it difficult to focus on anything else.

Playfulness twinkles in her eyes. I watch in shock as she stands up. She gives me a flirtatious look that makes me momentarily forget what century I'm in. She unbuttons her shirt, slowly pulling it off and revealing her voluptuous breasts covered only by her simple white undergarments. She pulls off her boots, then her culottes, and I stare in awe at her creamy white thighs. I swallow hard, my heart racing, but she doesn't even hesitate before she steps to the edge of the boat and jumps into the water.

I sit there for a moment, stunned, but then I'm moving before I even realize it. "Damn it, woman," I mutter to myself, but the grin on my face says everything I need to know. I take off my boots and follow her in, the cool water rushing around me when my head dips below the surface.

The river is quiet, peaceful, and the current is gentle. We swim for a while, laughing and splashing each other. She kicks water toward me, and I retaliate, sending a stream of water her way. Being with her is fun and easy, and I can't remember the last time I felt this carefree.

She swims over and treads water in front of me, her eyes holding mine with that heat that catches me off guard. I pull her closer, my hands on her waist, and my lips find hers. When we break apart, she looks up at me with that same teasing glint. I want more. I want to hold her body against mine forever, to find out what she feels like wrapped around me.

"Race you back to the boat." She's breathless, but before I can even respond, she's already swimming toward the canoe.

We reach the boat together, pulling ourselves back in, dripping wet but grinning like fools. The moonlight catches in her hair as she runs her fingers through it, water shimmering off her skin. For a second, I just watch her, wondering what it would be like to make her mine. I never expected this, but I damn sure don't want to leave it behind.

After we get dressed, we paddle back to shore, the boat scraping against the rocks when we reach the edge. I grab the rope and tie it to a nearby post. Our clothes stick to our skin, though they're beginning to dry in the evening heat.

I offer her my hand, and we walk back through the streets of Mesilla. I'm not sure how or why I ended up here, in 1875, but with Joanna's hand in mine, it suddenly feels like everything in the future might just be worth leaving behind.

10

LITTLE THINGS

Joanna

I wake slowly, the first morning light casting a warm glow around the room. My thoughts immediately drift to last night when Jake and I jumped into the Rio Grande, the cool water rushing around us as we laughed together. The kiss we shared, gentle and sweet, lingers in my mind, and I still feel his lips against mine. I smile to myself, remembering how everything about last night felt so right.

I rise from the bed, stretching my arms above my head. The cowhands headed back home last night, but Jake and I stayed the night at Shelby's house in Mesilla, and the quiet of the early morning is soothing. I throw my hair up in a bun and head out toward the kitchen, drawn by the smell of fresh coffee and sizzling bacon.

Shelby hums softly as she cooks. Her house is cozy and welcoming, filled with the familiar scents that make me feel like I belong here. Jake sits at the table, a cup of coffee in front of him, his eyes meeting mine as I enter.

"Good morning, Joanna." Jake smiles, his voice low and warm.

"Morning." I pour myself a cup of coffee and slide into the seat across from him. There's something about the early morning that feels peaceful, even more so with him here.

Shelby's busy with breakfast, and she glances over at us with a knowing smile. "So, how was last night? Seems like you two had a good time from how late it was when you strolled in." She winks, and I know she's watching to see how we react.

My cheeks warm slightly, but I don't hide the smile that creeps across my face. "It was a fun night."

She grins, clearly happy for me. "Good. You deserve it, Joanna. You work so hard." She places a plate of bacon, eggs, and biscuits in front of me, and I dig in, warmed to the core from her food and her kind words.

"Thank you so much for watching the animals and for breakfast, Shelby," I say between bites.

"Of course. Don't mention it." My friend waves her hand dismissively. "We've known each other since we were five years old. I can handle a couple of spare beds and a little breakfast for friends." She sets another plate in front of Jake, and he thanks her as well.

Outside, Margot, Ace, Lady, and Huck are playing in the garden, the soft sounds of barking and rustling filling the air. I glance out the window, watching the dogs chase each other around the yard, and for a moment, it feels like everything is just as it should be. Margot is limping, not as fast as usual, but it's clear she's getting better.

"You're doing all right though, Joanna?" Shelby's tone is gentle but serious. She looks at me with a mix of concern and care. "I know how hard the situation has been, with all there is to do on the ranch and the mounting bills. Are you taking care of yourself?"

I pause, meeting her gaze. It's rare for Shelby to ask questions like this, but I can feel the sincerity in her words. "I'm doing well." I hope I'm reassuring her because I'm not convincing myself. "It's just been a lot to handle, but I'm managing. Having Jake around has made things easier."

Shelby's expression softens. "Good. I'm glad. Just don't forget to slow down sometimes. You don't have to carry everything on your own." She joins us and digs into her eggs, which are the most delicious I've ever tasted.

I nod, appreciating her concern. "I know. Thanks, Shelby."

Jake places his cup down and looks between us. "I'll make sure she takes it easy, Shelby. No overworking, I promise." His voice is light, but I can hear the sincerity beneath it.

I smile at him, grateful for his reassurance. We finish breakfast, talking about the day ahead—getting back to the ranch, and taking care of the animals.

After we've eaten, Shelby walks with us to the door. "Take care of yourselves, both of you. You're always welcome here. You know that."

"Thanks, Shelby." I appreciate the warmth in her words. "I'm glad we could stay with you."

Jake smiles and gives her a nod. "We appreciate everything, Shelby. You've been wonderful."

With a final hug, we say our goodbyes and step out into the bright morning light. The dogs continue to play, and as I walk beside Jake toward the horses, a calm settles over me. The day stretches out ahead, and for the first time in a while, I feel ready for whatever comes next.

It's midday by the time Mesilla fades, miles behind us, its noise and commotion replaced by the relative silence of open land. The cattle drive is finally over, and while my shoulders and legs still ache from days on the trail, there's a lightness in my mood that has nothing to do with rest and everything to do with the way Jake's lips felt on mine last night.

He rides just ahead of me, Margot riding in front of him, upright this time, her stitches holding well. Jake keeps one protective hand on her the whole way.

When we get back on the ranch, we reach Ed's house first. He's working outside and tips his hat as his wife, Laurel, and two of their children wave from the front porch. Andy's house is nearby. His youngest child climbs the fence, hollering out a hello. We wave and laugh, and when Andy steps out, I give him a smile, glad he's home safe.

Jim's place is last, and his wife Constance stands on the porch, with their oldest two children, Chuck and Glory, running around the front yard. Jim must hear the commotion because he shuffles out the door. "Leg's doing much better," he calls.

"Good. If you need anything, let me know," Jake calls. I'm glad to see everyone made it home safely.

Jake and I turn toward my house, the dogs trotting alongside us. Huck runs ahead, Lady stays close to Chaco, and Ace drifts back and forth, not sure if he should run with the others or stay close to Jake. Margot thumps her tail weakly, and Jake murmurs something to her, low and gentle.

I can't stop smiling. He's a good man. He's thoughtful, capable, and someone I can rely on without thinking twice. The more time we spend together, the more I realize I like him, plain and simple.

I let out a contented sigh when my house and outbuildings come into view. We're finally home, and I'm thankful for it. When we reach the barn, we swing down from our horses, Jake moving carefully so Margot doesn't jostle. I take her to the house and lay her down in the kitchen while he takes care of Bridgit.

When I return to take care of Chaco, I catch Jake staring at me with a boyish grin. "What is it?" I ask.

"You're beautiful," he murmurs.

I snort. "I just got back from a cattle drive."

"A cattle drive that you ran," he replies. "You're such a good boss— and you're stunning."

A blush warms my cheeks against my will, and try not to show him how much I adore his attention.

We're finishing up with the horses, brushing them down and putting them out to graze, and I think of how nice it is to have someone here with me instead of doing it all alone. On the last few drives, I've had to come home to an empty house. Having Jake here makes it easier, and I can't help enjoying every moment of it.

The dogs gather near the barn, tired from the drive. We set out water and food in the feed pans, and they gulp it down.

I look up at Jake. "You can go give Margot some of those treats you have if you want. She's in the kitchen."

"Sure." He smiles and heads inside.

I stay outside, looking over the animals. The horses we didn't take on our trip with us are content. The goats wander the yard, and the chickens scratch at the dirt. Everything's in order. Kathleen, Constance, and Laurel took good care of things while I was gone. I let myself walk slowly and breathe deeply, taking in the sunlight and the tranquility of my ranch.

The cattle we drove to Mesilla are sold, and the rest are in their pastures. With the work finished, I start thinking about tonight. Maybe I'll fix a romantic dinner for the two of us, something hearty. After our long trip, it'll give us a chance to sit and enjoy the evening together.

As I walk back to the house with the money from the cattle I sold at Mesilla in my pocket, I feel a sense of relief. It won't cover everything I owe, but at least now I can start chipping away at my debts. I got more than expected this time, which was a wonderful surprise. There's still work to be done and debts to manage, but this coin makes it feel possible.

A sudden clatter of hooves makes me spin to look down the road. Dread washes over me when I see Chase Sawyer riding up. His ugly smirk is as infuriating as ever. "Joanna, we need to talk." He barely slows his horse when he starts barking at me.

"Not today, Mr. Sawyer. I don't have the patience or the energy for you." I glare up at him.

"Oh, Joanna, you're so sweet, thinking you have a choice in the matter. I came all this way. I'm not leaving, and you'll listen to every damn word I have to say."

I cross my arms and continue to glare.

"You know it'd be easier if you just married me. You could let go of all that debt on your back." He doesn't even bother to dismount before casting out another blasted proposal.

"I've told you time and again! I'm not marrying you, Chase Sawyer!"

He laughs, a short, bitter sound. "You think you can run a ranch alone? We all know the good Lord never intended women to even be allowed to own property. You can't handle it. You'll be forced to sell sooner or later."

"Leave!" I shout. "Get off my property, and this time, don't you dare ever come back!"

His horse stamps, but he doesn't retreat. "I'm not going anywhere until you understand—"

Chase stops mid-sentence. I turn to see Jake stepping out of the house, rifle raised. He doesn't yell. He doesn't even have to speak. He just stands there. A fondness heats my chest, and my heart hammers against my ribcage. Not with fear, but with pride.

The color washes out of Chase's face. He mutters, "You haven't seen the last of me. I'll be back, and next time… I'll *take* what I want." He nudges his horse and rides off.

I watch until the hoofbeats fade and then look at Jake. He lowers the rifle slowly, keeping his eyes on the path Chase took.

When I make my way to the porch, Jake sets his rifle down and turns to me. "Thank you." My voice cracks. He pulls me into his arms, and I rest my head against his chest, letting the tension of the last few minutes ease a little.

When we finally pull apart, he gathers the rifle, takes my hand, and leads me inside. "Why don't you let me draw you a bath?" he asks.

I don't argue, and Jake begins hauling water up from the well. I sit on the kitchen floor petting Margot as he heats the water over the stove and carries it to the tub. When it's full, he steps out of the room, leaving me alone. I undress and sink into the warm water.

I linger longer than I planned, thinking about Jake and the way he's always here, protective, thoughtful, and dependable. When I finally climb out, water dripping from my hair, the house smells delicious. I put on a clean dress and pin my hair up.

Then I round the corner into the kitchen, and Jake smiles at me. He's prepared the romantic dinner I was going to cook. Steak, potatoes, and roasted corn sits on my best plates, ready for us to consume.

I can't stop smiling. He's not just my friend, but he's a man who knows how to make me feel safe and cared for. There's no denying he's handsome, but it's the way he thinks ahead, and the way he does little things for me without a word that gets to me.

"I really appreciate you," I say. "Making dinner, preparing my bath, and handling Sawyer…."

He shakes his head and smiles. "Don't mention it. I take care of the people I care about."

I'm mid-bite when a sudden, frantic bellow cuts through the air. I freeze, straining to listen.

Jake frowns and cocks his head. "That doesn't sound right," he says.

We both jump to our feet, chairs scraping across the floor. I grab a lantern, Jake snatches a rifle, and we dash toward the sound.

We follow Huck and Lady to the northern pasture where one of my heifers is lying in the dirt, bawling, her flanks heaving. She's in labor, and something isn't right.

"Jake, she's struggling." My voice is tight with fear.

"I see," he answers calmly. "Help me keep her from panicking. Try to hold her still."

Normally, I'd take the lead, but Jake's got a way with injured animals, and right now, it's clear he knows what he's doing. My heart pounds as I crouch close, ready to help. He murmurs soothing words to the cow while adjusting the calf through her body. I can see right away that the little one's turned the wrong way, and the situation is about to get tricky. The heifer shifts and jerks, her muscles tensing, but Jake stays calm and focused. I grip her head, holding it firmly to keep her from thrashing, trying to match his composed demeanor, even as my mind races with the possibility of losing her and her calf.

Jake presses his hands hard against the cow's swollen belly, his fingers sinking into her tense flesh as he works to shift the calf into the right position. The cow groans, her body trembling beneath us, but she's too exhausted to resist. I press my palms into her side, helping to push, the bulge of the calf shifting under my hands. The muscles of her belly strain as we move it, the three of us becoming more anxious with each passing second. I hold my breath, wondering if this is even going to work, but finally, with one last push, the calf shifts into the right position.

The cow pushes one last time, and the calf slides free, slick and fragile. The heifer collapses, her body trembling with exhaustion, too worn out to move. The baby lies still for a moment, its tiny body twitching. I slide over beside the newborn bull-calf, gently rubbing him to help warm him up. His mother watches, her breath slow and deep. I continue to work on the calf, cleaning him, making sure he's safe while Jake tends to the mother cow.

"He's a healthy little guy," Jake says. "He'll be a strong one."

I let the calf nuzzle my hand, amazed at how small and perfect he is. "You made that look too easy."

He shakes his head. "You'd have done just as well. You've run this ranch long enough."

I glance from him to the cow and calf, feeling a rare stillness in the chaos of the day. He might be right, but it was better having him here.

I stand, brushing dirt from my dress. Jake looks at me, that easy grin lighting his face, and I can't stop the smile that spreads across mine. He gets to his feet, wiping his hands on a towel from his pocket.

"Should we let her nurse her baby?" I ask.

"Sure, but I'm coming out to check on them in an hour or so. I want to make certain momma cow is all right."

I realize, in that moment, just how much it matters to have someone by my side. Someone who's dependable, capable, kind, and watchful.

The heifer settles beside her calf, still panting, and Jake takes my hand. "Good work."

I nod, my heart still racing, and know that no matter what comes next, breech calves, cattle drives, debts, or Chase Sawyer—I'm not facing it alone anymore.

11

DEAL ME IN

No one's awake yet, and the morning's still cool, but I can feel the heat of the day already creeping in when I leave, the barn door creaking softly behind me. I check the bridle and give this fresh horse a gentle nudge forward. The trail ahead is rough, and the ride will test both of us, but I've ridden this way before.

I don't look back as I head down the dirt path. The trail stretches ahead, long and dusty, disappearing into the horizon like a promise I'm not sure I'll be able to keep.

Joanna is all I can think about. The way she pushes herself harder than anyone I've ever met, never asking for help, never taking credit for the hard work she puts in. I've never met anyone like her. She's strong and capable, and yet, there's a soft, feminine side to her, a vulnerability that gets buried beneath that wall she's built. She's headstrong, that's for certain. Somehow, that only makes me want her more.

I push the horse harder, kicking her into a lope, the wind whipping at my face. The road is rocky and uneven, but the mare handles it with ease. The trail is familiar, but that doesn't mean it's easy. The rocky terrain tests my endurance and forces me to keep my focus.

Out here all alone, one wrong move, and I could get hurt badly enough it could mean life or death.

The higher the sun rises, the hotter it gets. Sweat soaks through my shirt, but I don't slow down. I aim to be in Mesilla by dark, so I push on.

The trail suddenly curves, and I guide the horse around the bend, feeling the shift in the rocks beneath her hooves. The ground's uneven, almost sending her into a slide, but she regains her balance, and I keep my seat. The trail narrows ahead, leading toward the river crossing. The water's low, but the rocks underfoot are slick, so I slow the horse to a careful walk.

I get us up the far bank of the river and lead the mare over to a patch of dry ground. Sliding off, I grab my pack and pull out one of my few remaining protein bars. I reach into the side compartment for my water bottle, unscrew the cap, and take a long drink. I make myself comfortable on the ground in the shade of a small, scraggily tree.

I wonder if my phone will still turn on—not that it'll do me much good now. It's been sitting in my bag for weeks. I pull it out to check. It's odd that something I'm so used to having in my hand twenty-four/seven is so obsolete now. The screen flickers to life, and I check the battery. I've still got a little juice left. I turn it off again and tuck it back into the bag. Taking another drink from my water bottle, I start to unwrap the protein bar, but when I hear a rustling nearby, I look up and freeze. Just a few feet away, I see a rattlesnake, coiled and ready to strike.

Jumping to my feet, I grab my bag and swing back into the saddle. I heel the mare into motion, not wanting her to get bitten, and urge her into a fast gallop, leaving the snake behind. Getting bitten by a rattlesnake out here all alone would probably mean the death of me.

Hours later, I ride into Mesilla. The streets are bustling with activity. I pull up in front of a saloon, dismount, and tie the horse to a post near the water trough. She takes a long drink, and while she's at it, I hang a bag of oats I brought from the barn where she can reach it.

I walk into the saloon with one purpose: poker. Making my way to the back where a few men are already seated, I nod at the bartender and motion for a round of drinks for the table.

"Mind if I join you?" I ask.

One of the men glances at me, sizing me up. He nods after a moment. "If you've got the money."

I show them some of the coins I won weeks ago and take a seat, waiting for the dealer to shuffle the deck.

Fortunately, none of the men at this table are the fellas that I won money from the last time I played in Las Cruces. No one asks questions. They just deal me in. I don't look at anyone, choosing to focus on the cards in front of me. The men around the table are sizing me up. I can tell by the way they stare at me with narrowed eyes.

I learned long ago that poker's about more than the cards; it's about the people. Grandad Hank used to say that when I was a boy, and I know he was right. I've played plenty of hands since then, but it's different now. Back home, it wasn't just about winning. It was the sound of my dad, uncles, cousins, and Grandad all yelling at each other over the table, paired with the smell of Grandma's cooking. I'm not just missing poker right now. I'm missing home and my family, but I force my expression to remain neutral and watch them more than the cards. It's not the hand that matters. It's what my opponents are hiding.

The game goes on for a while. I win a few times and let the others have a hand or two to keep them from getting suspicious. By the time the pot's building, I've got most of their money in front of me. It's not luck. It's skill, and I've got it in spades.

Some of the men are getting irritated, glancing at me and then looking away, but they don't say anything. I've heard the whispers of "outsider" already, but no one's been bold enough to speak up yet.

The door opens quietly, but it's enough to make heads turn, and a teenage boy walks into the bar. He's probably about sixteen, maybe seventeen, but there's something about the way he carries himself, like he's been through too much to be scared of anyone or anything. It doesn't take long for people to notice him. His grin's too cocky, and his stance is too sure for someone his age.

The boy's got a gun on his hip, but it's the way he looks around that tells me he's not just some kid playing tough. He scans the room, his eyes quickly moving over everyone before settling on our game.

He steps up to the table, all confidence, like he's already part of the game. One of the men gives him a quick look and then nods toward an empty seat.

"Deal me in," the boy says.

The dealer does just that, and the boy eyes his hand without a word. The game picks back up.

The kid doesn't flinch when he wins a hand. Doesn't smile either. He plays it cool, even when the others get frustrated, and I can tell they're getting just as irritated with him as they were with me. They don't like losing, especially to someone as young as him.

The next hand is mine. I throw in a little more than I should, but I know they'll bite, and they do. The kid watches me, and I can see the wheels turning behind his eyes. He's trying to figure me out, but I don't give him anything.

I win the next hand, and by now the pot's big enough that there's more at stake than just a few dollars. The older men look at each other, muttering, but they don't get up. They're too deep in it and too proud to quit.

When I look at the kid again, he's got a smirk on his face. It's not the kind of smirk that says he's just here to have fun. No, he's playing for keeps.

I've already taken quite a bit of coin, and the kid's not backing down either. He wins one, I win one, and the money's starting to pile up. Every card that hits the table feels like it's pushing us closer to something bigger than just lady luck.

I decide to quit while I'm ahead. After my next win, I grab my winnings and stand up, but before I can take a step, one of the men's hands moves to the gun on his hip. He draws it, aiming straight at me, and the room goes dead silent.

The boy stands, too, his eyes narrowing as he looks at the man with the gun. He draws his own weapon, aiming it at the bastard.

"What's your problem, old man?" the kid says. "The gentleman didn't cheat. He's just good at playing the game."

The man's grip on his gun tightens, but he doesn't pull the trigger.

"You gonna let him walk out with your money, or you gonna end yourself here and now?"

The older man hesitates, looking between the kid and me. He lowers the gun, but the fire in his eyes doesn't go out.

I take the opportunity, grabbing my winnings and heading for the door, my back to the room. I don't look back.

As I step out into the warm evening, I hear the door behind me creak open again. I turn around just in time to see the boy emerge.

"Hey," he says. "Where'd you learn to play like that?"

"My grandad taught me," I say. "He taught me everything I know about poker and about life, too."

"I'll be damned," he mutters, almost to himself. "Granddad, huh? I didn't expect that." His lips curl into a half-smile. "I usually win, but I guess you're better than me."

"Hey, I appreciate your help back there, kid. That was really brave. I'm Jake Rawlins." I offer my hand.

"Henry McCarty," he says, returning a firm handshake.

The name rings in my head, but it takes me a second to put it together. I've heard the stories, and as a Texan, I know the history of the famous outlaw Henry McCarty. I'm standing here, face-to-face with a kid who's gonna make a name for himself. A kid they'll write stories and songs about.

"Guess I'll see you around, Billy," I say with a nod.

"Billy?" He asks. "I said my name is Henry."

"I know that. But I think folks are gonna call you Billy." I shrug.

The boy looks at me for a moment, then shakes his head with a smirk. "Billy the Kid, huh? Maybe that'll stick."

With a chuckle, I nod, walk over to the horse, swing up into the saddle, and head out into the moonlit night. Maybe I should warn him about Sheriff Garrett, but some parts of history are probably best left to play out.

12

BLESSED

I start the morning feeding the horses and gathering eggs, keeping my hands busy. Jake's been gone a day and a half, and he didn't leave a letter, or a word of where he might have gone. I go through the motions, but I can't shake the thought of him. Every time I pause, it's the same worry gnawing at me—is he safe? Is he ever coming back?

I fill the goats' water troughs, lifting the heavy buckets and letting the cold water spill in. They drink greedily, and I pat the back of the one closest to me, trying to ignore the knot in my chest. I keep telling myself I should be used to men coming and going, but this feels different. Maybe he didn't care for me quite as much as I care for him. He even took Ginger, one of my best mares, and I never would have guessed he'd be the type to steal a horse.

And yet... he left Ace here with me. That has to mean he's coming back, doesn't it? I can only hope.

The chickens cluck, pecking at the ground frantically where I've scattered their feed. I watch them, counting them to distract myself, but my eyes keep darting to the horizon. The wind carries no sound of hooves, no hint of his presence. I sigh and re-pin my hair, feeling helpless. I've tried to convince myself that he's fine, but the idea that he could be halfway to Houston by now tugs at me.

I sweep the porch next, and each movement feels mechanically hollow. My thoughts circle back to Jake constantly. Biting my lip, I force myself to finish my chores, the motions keeping me from unraveling completely.

By mid-day, I'm drenched in sweat and dirt. The work's done, but the feeling of emptiness lingers. I pause at the edge of my yard, looking out at the rolling land, hoping to catch a sign of someone coming up the road.

I'm washing the dinner dishes when I hear the rumble of hooves on the trail. My heart leaps into my throat, and I drop the cup I'm washing and run out the door as dust kicks up in the distance. A horse appears through the haze, and my stomach twists when I see it's Ginger—and Jake.

Once he's up by the house, he swings down from the saddle, a grin on his face as he saunters toward me. Part of me wants to smack him, but instead, I throw my arms around him and hold him close for a long moment. He kisses my forehead, and I remember how mad I am at him that he left without telling me where he was going. I push my palms against his chest. "Where have you been, Jake Rawlins?" I demand.

"I'm sorry, Joanna. I should've told you, but I knew you'd try to stop me." He pulls a large pouch out of his pack and holds it out to me. Narrowing one eye, I open it to see that it's filled with more than enough coins to cover every debt I owe and ease every worry. I stare up at him, unsure of what to say. He did this for me?

"I can't accept this." My voice sounds foreign even to me, trembling with disbelief. I shove the money back at him.

He shakes his head, that handsome smile curling at the corners of his lips. "I won it for you, and I want you to have it," he says.

Not sure what to say, I just stand there for a few moments, my mouth moving but nothing coming out. Finally, I tuck the pouch into my apron and embrace him again. My head spins at the thought of all the debts cleared, all the worries gone, and I can't help but wonder why anyone would do this for me.

"I… I don't know what to say," I manage, my voice cracking

"Then don't say anything. Just use it and get that jackass Chase Sawyer off your back."

For the first time in years, I feel like I can breathe without the edge of worry. I can pay the bills, keep the ranch, and maybe even start thinking about tomorrow without a pit burrowing into my stomach.

And yet, it isn't just the money. It's the kind and generous way he takes care of me without asking for thanks and without needing to be noticed. My heart stirs with admiration, gratitude, and love. He hasn't told me everything about himself, but I know enough about Jake Rawlins to understand the kind of man he truly is. They come few and far between.

Swallowing hard, I blink back the sting of tears, and nod once. "Thank you so much, Jake."

I step back, brushing my palms down my apron, trying to push away the tremor in my fingers. "Come on." I try to sound casual, even though my heart feels too full for me to breathe normally. "I'll draw you a bath and make you dinner this time."

He gives me a small, tired smile and nods. I hurry ahead, untying Ginger and leading her to the trough while Jake sits on the porch, loosening the straps on his pack. Ace sits at his feet, his tail wagging like Jake is his whole world.

We move inside the house, and I light the lanterns in the bedroom and fill the tub with hot water. I toss a towel over the edge of a chair and a bar of soap into the tub. "All right," I say, "the bath's ready. You can soak while I make your dinner."

As Jake gets cleaned up, I set the skillet on the stove and try to focus on a simple meal of fried ham and potatoes.

Just as I'm finishing up, Jake walks into the kitchen wearing clean clothes that fit him just right, and I have to stop myself from staring too long. He smells like the lavender soap I gave him, and his sandy hair is damp at the ends.

He sits at the table, and I place the food in front of him. "Here you are." I fill a glass with cool water and slide a glass of whiskey toward him as well. He nods his thanks but doesn't say much, just digs in. I bustle around the kitchen, getting him seconds, refilling his drinks, and pretending not to watch him eat, but I can't help sneaking glances.

"Aren't you going to eat?" he asks me a few minutes into his meal.

Shaking my head, I tell him, "I already did." It's not true, but I couldn't swallow a bite at this moment, not with my heart swelling so large it's filling me up completely.

When he finishes scarfing down the meal, he leans back, his hands resting on the table, and I step close and press my lips to his. It's soft and brief, but it carries trust, relief, and gratitude.

"I'll let you get to bed," I murmur. "And thank you—again."

"I'm glad I could help," is all he says as he stands and heads to the back of the house.

Quiet settles around the ranch like a soft blanket. In my room, I get ready for bed and pull the covers up, closing my eyes, but sleep doesn't come right away. My mind drifts over the day, over him, and over the way he's taken care of everything for me. I feel so damned lucky and so deeply blessed to have him here, to have him in my life. Finally, the thought carries me into sleep, where I'm lucky enough to dream of a long life with Jake by my side.

13

HAPPY HERE

The sun is hot on my neck as I watch Joanna guide the kids in roping practice. Constance and Jim's little ones are eager, their faces a mix of excitement and nervousness. I can't blame them. Roping a steer isn't easy, and they're all pretty green at it, but it's a skill they'll need to learn, and they're gonna learn it one way or another.

I've been here several weeks now, but there are still moments when I catch myself thinking, *How the hell did I get here?* And not in the context of time travel—but how did I become a ranch hand? I've come a long way from the chaos of 2025, and I feel like I'm starting to find my rhythm with these people. Teaching these kids feels natural, though it still surprises me how much I enjoy it. There's something about the way their eyes light up when they get a skill down that makes me forget how hard the work is.

Joanna moves between the children, showing them how to hold the ropes, making sure they're in the right position. She's got a way with them, patient and kind. They listen to her like they do their own mother. Her voice, soft but firm, carries over the wide stretch of dirt where we've set up the practice. We've got makeshift wooden steers ready to be roped. She encourages them kindly, and they beam at her. The children look up to her. Hell, I do, too.

"All right, kids," I call out, walking over to join them. "Let's see what you've got." I give one of the younger kids, Wally, a hand with his rope, showing him how to swing it, how to get the motion right.

Wally's grip is tight on the rope, his brow furrowed in concentration. I watch as he throws it, missing the "steer" by a wide margin. He kicks the dirt in frustration, but I can tell he's not giving up.

"Close, Wally." I clap him on the back. "Your form's good, but you gotta aim for the neck. You're aiming too low. Let's try again."

Joanna moves up beside me, offering her encouragement. "You can do it, Wally." Her voice is soft and warm. She steps back, letting him take another shot. The next throw is a little better, and though he misses again, he's clearly starting to get the hang of it.

I turn to the older kids, watching as they try their hands at roping. Chuck, Jim's oldest, looks confident. He swings the rope with ease, but when he throws it, he's too slow. The rope lands on the steer's back, but not around its neck.

"You're getting there, Chuck," I say, giving him a nod. "But you gotta follow through with the throw. You're too stiff. Loosen up."

He repositions, and the rope flies through the air with more confidence. This time, it lands just over the steer's horns. He pulls the rope tight, and for a second, I think he's done it, but the rope falls, and then slips free.

"Good attempt, though." I walk over to him, patting his shoulder. "Next time, stay low when you follow through."

Joanna's voice cuts in, full of praise. "You almost had it, Chuck! That was the best throw yet."

The kids all work hard, pushing themselves, their faces lit with determination. I can feel the weight of the responsibility on my shoulders, but I wouldn't trade this for anything. Watching these kids grow, watching them learn—I feel like this is where I'm meant to be.

After a few more attempts, Glory, Jim's nine-year-old daughter, finally ropes the steer, and all the kids cheer, rushing to pat her on the back. Their grins are wide, and I know this moment will stick with them for a while.

"Good job, everyone." I start to give Glory a high-five but remember she doesn't know what that is, so I pat her head instead. Then, I look over at Joanna. She's smiling, pride evident in her eyes. She's been so strong through all of this, and seeing her here with the kids, teaching them alongside me, lets me know I've found something real here.

After the roping lesson, Joanna and I move around the corral together, checking fences and feeding the animals. She's humming softly, and I catch myself smiling at the sound. That's when we notice the bull-calf, born just a few days ago, isn't with his mother. I scan the field but don't see him.

"The little guy's gone," I say.

"I don't see him anywhere." She lifts a hand to shield her eyes from the sun. "I'm sure he didn't wander too far."

"I'll ride out and see if I can find him."

She nods, distracted as she continues to look around, and I head for the barn. Ginger snorts when I pull her out of her stall and saddle her up, swinging up, and heading out.

Dust and grit sting my eyes as I ride across the dry pasture, scanning the ground, looking for tiny hoofprints, trying to see if the calf passed this way. Then the sound of hooves pounds behind me. I turn around to see a horse is coming fast, its rider leaning forward, gun leveled. It's that bastard Chase Sawyer.

Before I can react, he fires directly at me. I yank Ginger to the side. She bucks and scrambles, hooves slipping on loose dirt. She stumbles, then crashes to the ground, taking me with her. Pain lances up my side as she lands on top of me, and dirt fills my mouth. I close my eyes and try to catch my breath as soon as he rolls off me.

Sawyer chuckles. "Got 'I'm," he says. He must assume I'm dead, either from the horse or his shot. The sound of hooves pounding away lets me know he's not getting close enough to see I'm still breathing.

I struggle to get up, twisting my arms, trying to get leverage, but every movement sets a fresh wave of pain through my ribs. Ginger thrashes around, finally bolting off into the distance, leaving me bruised, battered, and alone. I'm left sprawled in the dirt, gasping as pain tears through my side. I try to rise, but my body won't cooperate. All I can do is lie here and look up at the sky, praying Joanna is all right and will come looking for me soon.

Hours pass, and the sun climbs overhead and keeps going, baking me into the ground beneath. My body aches in places I've never even felt before. My mouth is dry, my tongue thick, and every swallow hurts. Heat blurs the edges of my vision, and I try to stay focused. Joanna will notice I'm not back yet and come looking for me. Or maybe one of the cowboys will ride out, follow Ginger's tracks, and see me lying here. I cling to that hope as the light starts to soften because the alternative is being stuck out here after dark, hurt and alone, with no water and no way to move.

To think, just a few hours ago, we were having fun with the kids, and now, I'm out here alone, waiting to be found—or to die.

Finally, I hear a horse coming and lift my head. A rider breaks over the rise and heads straight toward me. It isn't until she's close that I realize it's Joanna. She dismounts and crosses the last few steps fast.

"Jake!" she calls. Her voice is sharp, cutting through the pain and haze. She kneels beside me, checking my body for injuries. I can't stop groaning, the pain radiating through my chest, ribs, and legs. I open my mouth to tell her what's wrong, but no words come out.

"Stay still." Concern is evident in every word. Her hands hover over my chest as if she's unsure where to touch me without causing more pain. "You're hurt bad." She scans me quickly and then shakes her head. "I can't move you on my own."

I try again to say something, but my body refuses to obey.

"I'm going for help," she continues, a firmness in her tone that gives me strength. "I'll be back as fast as I can."

With that, she's off, disappearing toward the horizon, leaving me behind, stuck in the heat with nothing but the sound of my own ragged breathing.

I must black out for a bit because it seems like she's back in no time at all. My vision is blurry, but I recognize Ed and Andy's voices. One of them pulls the wagon to a stop and quickly jumps down to help the other. They lift me carefully and lie me in the wagon bed. Every movement sends a sharp pain through me, but I grit my teeth and try to stay still.

Once I'm settled, Joanna climbs into the bed beside me, sitting close. Cradling my head in her hands, she lifts a canteen to my swollen mouth. I want to guzzle it down, but I have to settle for a few sips.

"I'm so sorry I didn't find you sooner, Jake. I was in the barn dealing with a snake nest and didn't realize how much time had passed until Ginger came back alone." I can hear the guilt in Joanna's voice.

I can't respond. I try to smile, but it does nothing to erase the grimace on her pretty face.

One of the fellas climbs back up to the driver's seat, taking the reins, and the wagon lurches forward, slowly rolling over the rough ground.

"Just breathe, Jake," Joanna says softly, her voice calm. "We'll be home in a minute."

By the time we reach the house, I'm shivering from shock. I'm battered and bruised, but I'm still alive. Ed and Andy lift me as carefully as possible. I can't move on my own, and every breath feels like a fight. They carry me inside, moving quickly, and I can't help but wince at each shift of their grip, the pain spiking with each jarring step.

Once we reach the bedroom, they lower me onto the bed as gently as they can. My body protests the movement, and I barely hold back a scream, but I can't bring myself to make a sound beyond the ragged breaths I can barely manage.

Joanna's next to me, a glass of water in her hand, helping me sit up, as she presses the glass to my lips. The water is cool going down, dulling the ache in my throat the few sips from the canteen didn't alleviate.

"Easy now," she says. "Just drink. I'll take care of you."

"What the hell happened, Jake?" Andy demands.

I take a shaky breath, struggling to get the words out. My voice is raspy and soft. I hardly recognize it. "Sawyer. He shot at me. Spooked Ginger, and she went down. She fell right on top of me." Each breath I take is shallow and painful as I force the words through a clenched jaw. "I didn't see it coming. I didn't have a chance to react before she pinned me."

Joanna's nostrils flare at the news, but she takes a moment to think before she speaks. Her hands move over me, pressing against bruised flesh to check for broken bones. "I thought we'd taken care of him," she finally mutters, but I know she's not talking to me. She's just thinking out loud.

"Honestly, for a while, I didn't think I was gonna make it," I rasp, trying to push through the pain and keep talking.

She pauses, her eyes moving up to mine. "We'll get you through this, Jake. You're going to be just fine."

Ed's eyes are narrowed, his face scrunched. He paces the room, his hands clenching into fists. "That damn bastard Sawyer. He thinks he can bully everyone, pushing people around like he owns the whole damn world." He spits out the words like they're poison.

Andy stands by the window, looking out as if he might charge after Sawyer right then and there. "No one should have to put up with his bullshit. He's crossed the line too many times now." His voice is low, but the fury is clear. "We need to put an end to that shitheel. I have half a mind to go teach him a lesson right now."

Joanna stands, her expression calm. "I agree with you both, but not tonight." Her gaze softens just a bit, meeting Andy's. "Thank you for everything. Both of you. But Jake needs rest. We'll discuss what to do about Sawyer tomorrow, after we've all had a chance to calm down."

Ed and Andy exchange looks, the fire in their eyes still burning, but they nod, stepping back toward the door. "We'll see you in the morning," Ed says before he and Andy head back home.

As I lie here, bruised and battered, every breath still a struggle, I can't help but think how close I came to dying. I almost became another ghost in the desert wind. But now, I'm here with Joanna, her hand wrapped around mine, and I know she's not letting go.

Joanna stays with me into the night, cleaning and bandaging my scrapes and keeping the water coming. She brings me whiskey to dull the pain, and though it burns going down, it helps take the edge off. Her hands are gentle as she adjusts the blankets, making sure I'm as comfortable as I can be. I'm too worn out to say much, too tired to do anything but let her take care of me. Each time I start to drift, I feel her hand on mine, a reminder that I'm not alone. Finally, the pain eases enough, and the exhaustion takes over. Sleep pulls me under, and for the first time in hours, I don't feel like I'm hanging on by a thread.

* * *

OVER THE NEXT WEEK, THE PAIN STARTS TO FADE IN WAVES. Thankfully, none of my bones were broken, but my body is a patchwork of blue and green bruises in various phases of healing. Every morning when I wake up, I feel it less, and with each passing day, it becomes easier to move.

Joanna's been relentless in her care, bringing me warm meals, helping me stretch out my muscles, and making sure I drink enough water. She's always here, gently checking my bandages, helping me sit up to drink water and broth, and bringing me whiskey to dull the sharpest parts of the pain. Her presence is like the sun breaking through the clouds, kind and patient, until I can see clearly again.

By the eighth day, I'm moving around more. At first, it's just small movements: shifting in bed, sitting up without wincing, stretching my arms out to ease the stiffness. Joanna stays close, always ready to help me if I need it. I can tell by the way she watches me, and how she scrunches her cute little nose when I push too hard, that she wants to protect me from doing more damage.

"Don't push yourself too hard," she says one afternoon, watching me as I walk slowly around the house, leaning heavily on the furniture. "You're healing, but you're not fully there yet."

On the tenth day, I decide to try to walk outside. I move at a snail's pace at first, each step tentative. Ace watches me from the porch, his ears perked, his tail wagging as if he's waiting for me to take him out on a hunt.

"Hang on, boy," I mutter. He's been restless without me.

Joanna and Andy are sitting on the porch talking when I step outside. The moment they see me, both of them stand, looking surprised.

"You sure you should be out here, Jake?" Andy's eyes dart to my ribs.

"I'm fine," I lie. I'm far from it.

Joanna's gaze softens, but she doesn't scold me. Instead, she looks back at Andy and gives a small nod. "Let him move. He's been cooped up for too long."

I shuffle over to Ace and pat his head. My dog's been nothing but patient with me, even when I couldn't give him the attention he deserves. "We'll get back out there soon, buddy."

"When are you gonna teach us how to hunt with that dog?" Andy asks, leaning against the porch railing, clearly intrigued by the idea.

I look up at both Andy and Joanna. "You interested?"

Her face brightens, a smile tugging at her lips. "I've never gone quail hunting before. I've wanted to since the first time you described it, though."

I'm a little surprised, but the thought of getting out and hunting with Ace is exciting.

"You sure? You'll need to keep up," I tease, knowing full well that it's me that will have problems keeping up at the moment. "Let's go. Ace needs the exercise, and we won't need to go far."

"I don't know if it's a good idea for you to be so far away from the house right now," Joanna warns.

I chuckle. "I'm sure the two of you can help me stumble back if I get ahead of myself."

Andy says he's going to go get Ed and Jim, and I take a rest in a rocking chair while Joanna gets her rifle ready. An hour or so later, we head off toward the closest pasture. It's slower than usual for me, but the excitement is contagious. The fresh air feels good, and I can already feel my muscles loosening, the pain in my ribs fading a little more.

When we reach an open meadow of tall grass, I give my bird dog the command. "All right, Ace, find 'em," I say, and the dog takes off, weaving through the field, his body sleek and his mind focused.

We walk slowly behind him, still cautious but feeling the familiar pull of the hunt. Ace stops suddenly, his nose to the ground. He's got a scent.

"That's it." I point to the spot. "He's found them."

Joanna's eyes fill with curiosity. "How do you know for sure?"

"He'll freeze like that when he's on point," I explain. "Watch him. He's showing us where the birds are."

We move in slowly, keeping quiet as I get closer to where Ace is pointing. I take a few careful steps forward, my eyes on the brush ahead. Then, with a quick jab of my boot, I kick up the covey. In an instant, the air fills with the frantic beat of wings as the quail explode from the underbrush.

Without hesitation, they all raise their rifles and fire. The crack of gunshots rings out, and a handful of birds fall about fifty yards away. I watch in amusement, not yet ready to have the butt of a rifle lodged against my aching shoulder.

Ace is already on the move, cutting through the meadow as he sniffs the ground, tracking the fallen birds. He works fast, each movement with purpose, his nose working overtime to find every last one. Within moments, he's back, trotting proudly with a bird in his mouth. He drops it into my hand before heading off again to fetch the next one. One by one, he returns, each bird gently held in his mouth, his tail wagging with pride in his work.

The fellas watch in awe, impressed by how smoothly Ace works. "Hell, that's something," Jim mutters, shaking his head with a grin. "Never saw a dog work like that."

Joanna laughs, still watching Ace as he drops the last bird into her open palm. "Good boy, Ace! I'll give him credit. He's got skills. I'm used to working cattle dogs, and I never imagined there were dogs that could do this. I wonder if Margot could learn."

I nod, proud of Ace and how well he's doing. "He's a hell of a dog, but I'm sure Margot could learn, too. She just needs to watch Ace and learn a few simple commands."

By the time the sun begins to set, I'm feeling better than I have in days. I'm tired, but I feel good. I've got my dog, my new friends, and have had the opportunity to teach them something I love.

Joanna and I make our way back to the house, Ace running beside us. The others have gone on home, so it's just the three of us now. As we walk in silence, I can't help but think about how this isn't truly my home. I'm not back in 2025, and every time I turn around, I'm faced with some new danger, some new obstacle. But in this moment, with Joanna at my side and Ace following close, I feel something I never expected. Maybe it's not perfect, and maybe it's not the life I imagined, but damnit, I'm happy here.

14

LOVE

Joanna

The afternoon sun is high in the sky as Jake and I ride into Las Cruces. The town, filled with activity today, is vastly different from the quiet of my ranch. Horses' hooves clatter against the dirt street. Voices hum from all directions, and the bustle of people moving from one shop to the next fills my ears. I never realized how much of the errands I used to have to do alone, and now that Jake's here, I'm thankful for his presence at my side.

Our first stop is the general store. The door creaks as we enter, and the smell of dry goods, leather, and flour fills the air, mixing with the faint scent of tobacco.

The shopkeeper, Mr. Roberts, looks up from behind the counter, his mustache twitching as he offers a polite nod. "Miss Joanna," he greets me, his voice warm but professional. "What can I do for you today?"

"I've come to pay my bill," I say proudly, pulling the small leather pouch from my belt, which holds the money Jake won for just this purpose.

Mr. Roberts smiles brightly as I hand him the money I owe. "Very good, Miss Calloway. I'm certainly glad things are looking up for you, my girl."

I watch him stamp **PAID** in his ledger, and the relief of getting this task done washes over me. I smile in thanks. "Mr. Roberts, I appreciate your patience with me."

He nods. "Of course, Joanna. Glad to have helped. Take care now." He returns to his work, and we leave, heading down the street to Harper's livery. Jake and I stop to chat with Basil Harper, who runs the place, keeping a careful watch on the horses. My bill here is small compared to the general store's, but the care of my ranch's animals is vital, and Basil has always been good to me whether I need a horse shoed while I'm in town or need to keep a horse overnight.

Next, we head to the blacksmith's, where I pay for the nails, tools, and repairs we've needed over the last month. I always dread seeing that bill, but it's one of those necessary costs of owning land and livestock, and it's unavoidable all the same. Jake walks next to me, and I take his arm as we move toward the final stop.

"Ready to pay the taxes?" I ask, keeping my voice light, though inside, I'm tense. Taxes were never something I enjoyed dealing with.

"Not really." Jake chuckles. "But it has to be done."

We reach the clerk's office, a modest stone building tucked at the corner of the town square. Inside, the air is thick with the smell of ink and paper, and the faint sound of quill pens scratching on parchment fills the room. The clerk's secretary, a thin woman with round spectacles, looks up as we enter.

"Good afternoon, Miss Calloway. Here to pay your taxes?"

I nod, placing the envelope of gold coins on the counter. She takes it, counting the coins with meticulous care. A slight smile tugs at the corner of her lips as she makes a note in her ledger.

"All paid up for the year, dear," she confirms. "You're all squared away."

I breathe out a sigh of relief. "Thank you."

With all the bills and taxes paid, I feel a weight lift from my shoulders. Jake and I walk back out onto the street toward the horses, the bright sunlight now seeming a little warmer, a little more welcoming. I look over at him, and he smiles, his arm slipping around my shoulders. The town continues to hum around us, but for the moment, it feels like it's just Jake and me, moving forward together.

It feels good to hold my head up high and breathe easily.

* * *

THE DAY AFTER OUR TRIP TO PAY UP OUR BILLS, I'M FINISHING UP WITH the chores, checking horseshoes, when I see that Bridgit needs one of hers replaced. Thankfully, this is work I can do myself this time without having to take her to the livery. I set to work. She's being a little stubborn, so I'm taking my time, making sure she's comfortable. I hear footsteps and look up to see Jake.

"Need a hand?" he asks.

"Well, if you don't mind holding her head while I finish this, I wouldn't turn down the help."

He moves over, taking Bridgit's head gently in his hands. "Sure, but if I get kicked, you owe me a beer," he jokes with that mischievous grin that always makes my cheeks flush.

I roll my eyes, trying to hide my grin. "We'll be lucky if I don't have to patch you up again after this. First, you get struck by lightning. Then, Ginger falls on you. What's next, Jake? You planning to wrestle a bear?"

I glance up to see a sheepish smile on his handsome face. "Only if you're around to bandage me up afterward."

I giggle. "You sure do seem to get yourself into trouble. It's a good thing you've got someone here to help you out."

He laughs and hands me the tool I need to finish the job.

When I'm done with Bridgit's shoe, I look up at him. "You're getting better, though."

He grins. "I feel much better today."

That spark between us, the one that's been growing since he first showed up here, sizzles between us. Releasing the horse, I walk toward him, stopping just in front of him, and rest my hands against his chest, pressing a quick, gentle kiss to his lips. He slides his arms around my waist, pulling me closer, and the kiss deepens.

Releasing me, he pulls back just enough to look at me, his hands still resting on my waist. "I'll go start dinner."

I take a deep breath, not ready to let go of the warmth still lingering between us. But he's right to stop before things get too heated. "I have just a few more chores," I reply. "I'll be right in."

He nods before turning toward the house. I watch him walk away, the imprint of his touch still on me, and for a moment, I slow down to savor the feeling of being wanted—of being cared for so deeply.

I finish the last of the chores, checking the fence line in the pasture closest to the house, and giving the animals a final once-over. My thoughts keep drifting to Jake. I'm strolling back to the house when a realization sets in. It's not just that I'm falling for him—I'm already in love with him. I've known him for a while now, seen every side of him, and I can't deny it anymore. There's nothing about him I don't adore.

He's protective and brave, never hesitating when someone or something needs his help. He's a damn hero when the situation calls for it. But there's another side to him, too, one I've come to admire just as much. He's patient and kind, always willing to lend a hand, to teach, and to make things easier for everyone around him. Then, there's his vulnerable side, the one that still surprises me sometimes. The way he lets me take care of him, lets me help him when he's been knocked down, when he's hurting and needs someone to patch him up.

I've never been one to romanticize people, but damn, Jake is difficult *not* to love. The more I see of him, the more I realize I've never met anyone like him. Maybe that's what love is. It's not a sudden feeling, not a spark that catches fire in an instant. It's the way he fits into my life, into my world, and makes everything better.

I walk into the house, ready to grab some food and finish my day, but then I stop in my tracks. The place is spotless. Jake's been busy. There's a fire crackling in the hearth, casting a glow over the room, and the table is set. A small candle flickers in the center, next to a vase holding fresh flowers. The delicious smell of savory meat cooking fills the air.

He's standing near the stove, stirring something in a pot. He turns around with that handsome smile of his. "Dinner's almost ready."

I stand there for a moment, awestruck, taking it all in. The work he's put into the meal, the way he's transformed this old dusty house into something clean and welcoming—I don't even know when he had the time to do it all.

"Jake?" My voice catches a little. "This is amazing."

He shrugs, looking a bit embarrassed. "Figured I'd do something to repay you for nursing me back to health."

I walk over to him, placing a hand on his arm. "I appreciate you so much."

"Come sit down." He gestures to the table. "I made your favorite."

I smile and take a seat, warmth washing over me from the inside out. Jake is here with me, doing everything he can to make me feel special—that's what love is.

The meal is perfect, and just what I need. The flavors of the beef, mashed potatoes, and vegetable melody come together so well, and I can tell Jake put a lot of effort into it. We eat slowly, savoring each bite, laughing and teasing each other. It's not just the food that makes the evening; it's how comfortable we feel together.

Afterward, we both pitch in with the dishes. I wash and Jake dries. Once everything is cleaned up, I turn to face him. He steps closer, his hands gently cupping my face as he leans in, his lips meeting mine. The kiss is soft and sweet at first, but when I kiss him back, I feel the urgency of desire and kiss him more passionately.

I pull away, and clarity unlike anything I've ever experienced before settles over me. "Come to my bedroom," I whisper.

He doesn't hesitate. I take his hand and lead him down the hall. Once we reach my room, he kisses me again. I've never done this before, but he's patient and slow, making sure I'm comfortable with each piece of clothing that falls to the floor.

When I stand before him, completely bare, Jake looks me over, his gaze filled with desire. "You're so beautiful, Joanna." His voice is deep, almost a growl, and I don't feel the least bit embarrassed to reveal everything to him.

Biting my bottom lip, I drink in the sight of his sculpted body. Every muscle ripples when he moves toward me. My breath staggers, and when he draws me toward him, I clutch his biceps to keep my feet beneath me.

His lips find mine as I slide my hands up his chest, his muscles firm beneath my fingertips. I let them roam, memorizing every inch of him as he deepens the kiss.

He pulls back for a moment, his breath hot against my skin, and then his lips trail down to my neck, kissing me gently at first before moving lower, trailing down the curve of my chest. I let out a moan, savoring every touch.

We fall onto the bed, tangled in each other, hands moving over skin, exploring, wanting each other more than anything. He kisses and nips at my skin, his mouth moving from one breast to the other. The sensation is overwhelming, unlike anything I've ever experienced before.

When his hand finds my folds, he moves with precision, making me ache for more. I lean into him, the tension growing, feeling every pulse of desire, as he coaxes me closer to my peak.

"Jake, take me," I gasp between moans. "I want you to."

He looks up at me, positions himself between my legs, lines the head of his cock up with my opening, and presses inside of me, sliding up and down with purpose. It hurts a bit at first when he's completely inside me, but when he pumps his hips, my body reacts instinctively, and I grab his biceps to hold on, my body moving in time with his.

"You feel incredible," he murmurs, hovering above me, love shining in his green eyes.

My body quakes. I lift my legs higher, giving him a deeper angle and he thrusts harder and harder until I feel as if I might come undone.

"Jake, don't stop," I beg as he drives me to ecstasy.

Every inch of me is on fire, my breath quickening as I move with him, the tension in my body building with each thrust. I can feel the pressure deep inside growing stronger and more intense until I'm barely holding on. I tighten around him, desperate, my pulse racing as he drives me closer, and then, with a final rush of sensation, my body trembles, and I'm lost to the world, my vision blurring as the pleasure crashes through me, leaving me completely enraptured by him.

He tenses against me, his breath ragged, the urgency in his movements matching the beating of my heart. Jake buries himself inside me one last time with a low groan that sends a thrill through me. His deep, hot release spills inside of me just before he shudders. We both hold on, caught in the aftershocks, bodies pressed together as the world slowly comes back into focus, leaving us breathless and satisfied.

We stay wrapped around one another, both of us too caught in the moment to move. His heartbeat still thunders against mine. I run my fingers along his back, and a strange sense of peace settles over me. He gently brushes my hair back from my face, and when I look up, his eyes meet mine, full of an unspoken connection that's never been more undeniable.

I think... he loves me, too.

15

MANHANDLED

When I wake up, Jake's not in bed with me, but I smell sizzling ham, potatoes, and freshly brewed coffee. All those scents make my stomach growl with hunger. Before I move, I take a contended breath. I don't think I've ever been happier.

In the kitchen, dawn light streams through the open window, giving Jake a soft glow. He's wearing my apron, flipping fried potatoes.

"Good morning to you, Miss Calloway." He glances over his shoulder with that cute smile of his. "Your table awaits, my lady."

"That smells incredible," I manage to say, a little overcome with gratitude. He doesn't have to take care of me, and yet, he always does. Yet, I hesitate. Surely, I can help somehow.

Reading my mind, he shakes his head. Jake's grin widens, and he gestures toward the chair at the small table. "Sit. I've got breakfast covered. You're taking the day off."

I laugh softly, incredulous. "The day off?"

"Yep." Turning back to the stove, he continues. "I'll cover my chores and yours. I'll handle everything today. You go spend the day with Kathleen, Constance, Laurel, and all the kids. You've earned it."

My heart feels so full. He really means it. He's taking the weight of the ranch off my shoulders, even if just for one day, giving me permission to breathe and to go enjoy myself and be like one of the girls. I feel a little light-headed at how good he is to me, how carefully he watches over me without me having to ask.

"Jake…" I start, unsure how to put my feelings into words.

"Don't argue and don't thank me, pretty lady." He walks to the table and slides a plate in front of me. "Eat, and don't you worry about a thing."

With a sigh and a shake of my head, I take my seat and dig in. In this moment, I feel completely smitten. With the way he looks at me, the way he anticipates what I need, the way he makes me feel like I can just exist and be taken care of… I can't remember the last time someone did this for me without me asking, but it was probably my mother.

"You're sure?" I know what he'll say, but I can't help but ask again.

"Absolutely." Jake sits across from me with his plate loaded. He meets my gaze, and my stomach flips. God, he's so handsome. "Go. Have fun. Laugh. Spend time with your friends. I've got it covered."

My chest swells with gratitude. How did I get so lucky? He sips his coffee as if he hasn't shown me more kindness than anyone else in the world.

Watching him, I realize how much I've come to depend on him—not just for help around the ranch, but for the way he makes life feel. When he's around, I not only feel safe and cared for, I feel lighter. My shoulders lift, my face lights up, and I can breathe without feeling like a load of bricks rests on my chest.

I eat slowly, savoring the food but mostly enjoying my time with him. Is it possible I could grow to love him even more? It doesn't seem possible.

Later in the morning, I lean against the wooden counter in Kathleen's kitchen, the smell of fresh bread filling the cabin, warm and comforting, mingling with the sound of laughter from the children in the yard. All of us womenfolk are working together baking bread.

Conversation flows around me, but I can't seem to focus on anything except the images of last night swirling in my mind.

Jake's hands on me, the feel of his body against mine, and the way he looked at me while we made love…. I smile to myself, barely able to contain my love-struck bliss. How can I? The way he makes me feel, the way my heart races when I think about him, it's like nothing I've ever experienced.

"Joanna, are you with us?" Kathleen's voice brings me back to the kitchen.

"Sorry, I was just thinking." My cheeks warm. I'm certain they all know exactly who I'm thinking about—if not what.

"Oh, we can tell." Constance winks at me. "You've got that look. This wouldn't have anything to do with a certain new field hand, would it?

I can't help but laugh. "You know it does," I admit. "I… I think I'm in love with him."

The room falls quiet for a beat, and my heart races again, just from saying the words aloud.

Kathleen looks up from her kneading with a knowing look. "Young love," she says with a quiet smile. "It's a wild, natural thing, isn't it?"

Laurel chuckles, pressing down hard into the dough and pulling. "I remember when I fell in love with Ed. Everything about it felt thrilling and fun. The way he looked at me back then… it was like nothing else in the world existed except for the two of us. It's a kind of magic, really."

I nod, joy blooming inside me at the thought. I've never been in love before, and I never thought I'd find someone who makes me feel like I'm the center of his world. He's not just my lover. He's my partner and my best friend.

"I feel the same way," I whisper, as though saying it too loudly might make it disappear. "It's like it was just always meant to be."

"Sounds like a fairytale," Constance muses, pausing with the flour-dusted rolling pin in her hand. "So when's the wedding?"

We all giggle, and I start to picture a small ceremony.

Kathleen glances over at me, her gaze warm and wise. "Love isn't always easy though, Joanna. But it's worth it. You have to give it your all, even when it feels like it might break you. That's the beauty of it."

"I think it's worth the risk." I smile. "I really do."

I catch the glances exchanged between the women, their expressions full of approval. They've all been here; they've all known this feeling, and somehow, that makes me less nervous about the path I'm walking with Jake.

As I look down at the dough in front of me, I realize that everything's changed, and yet everything's the same. I'm still me. I'm still here, on my ranch, but in a way, I feel like I'm beginning something new, something real with Jake, and I wouldn't have it any other way.

I leave Kathleen's house just before sunset, a peaceful calm settling over me. The bread, warm and freshly baked, is tucked neatly into the cloth bag hanging at my side. The other women are still inside, chatting and tending to their children, but I'm eager to head home—to Jake. It was a wonderful day, but it will be an even better evening.

About halfway home, the path narrows as it winds through a thick patch of mesquite trees. The canopy overhead casts everything in shadow, the light dimming as I move deeper into the thicket. My mind is on Jake, not on my route. It's so familiar, I could walk it blindfolded.

Rustling in the tree line draws my attention. I turn, but before I can even see what's happening, strong arms wrap around me. Rough hands grab my wrists from behind, yanking me off balance.

I try to twist away, but the grip on my wrists tightens. The bread bag falls from my shoulder as another man steps out from behind me, grabbing my legs and lifting me off the ground. I kick and struggle, screaming for help, but it's no use. They drag me off the path, pulling me into the trees. I haven't gotten a good look at their faces because of the shadows and their swiftness of their attack, but I think I know who at least one of them is.

Panic rises in my whole body. "Let go of me!" I scream, but a hand slaps over my mouth, silencing me before I can make another sound.

"Quiet now," Sawyer growls. I'd recognize his voice anywhere.

Like a snake, it slithers through my ears, cold and cruel. The other man, behind me, wraps a rope around me, binding my arms to my hips. He takes his hand off my mouth, and his grip on my arms tightens.

"What do you want?" I demand.

His evil laugh echoes in the woods. "You'll find out soon enough, sweetheart." With that, he ties a bandana around my mouth, muting me. I struggle, but it's no use.

They shove me into the back of the wagon. Sawyer binds my feet. I kick at him, but with my arms in this unnatural position, I can't get any leverage. I don't recognize the other man, but he's even stronger than Sawyer. I'm simply no match for them.

Fear fills me. I know exactly what this bastard has in mind. I need to escape now, before it's too late. With the bandana around my mouth, I can't speak, but I do manage to make a high-pitched whistling sound, hoping Margot will hear me. If only I could call out for Jake.

Sawyer snarls. "Make another noise, little girl, and I'll shoot you." With that, the two of them get in the wagon, and it jolts forward, creaking with every bump as it makes its way through the forest. I rotate my wrists, trying to loosen the rope, but my arms are bound tight to my sides.

We climb higher into the hills, the ground rough and uneven beneath us. Hours pass, and the path winds deeper into the dense woods, the trees thickening with each turn. It's dark now, the last traces of light swallowed by nightfall. I try to make sense of where we are, but the isolation and gloom set in, and I realize we're too far from anything familiar. I can't lift my head much, but I haven't seen a house or another wagon. Even if I could scream, it wouldn't help.

Finally, after what feels like an eternity, the wagon slows. I see a cabin in the distance, small and secluded, tucked between the trees. The dread in my stomach deepens.

Chase Sawyer pulls me from the wagon and throws me over his shoulder. He carries me into the cabin and dumps me onto a bare bed. I'm met by the cold stares of three new men I don't recognize, watching me with cold, hungry eyes. The man from the wagon follows us in, and panic rises in my chest as I realize I'm trapped with five men, and no way out.

I'm still bound, my arms aching, but he yanks the bandana off my mouth. Sawyer looms over me, his expression hard and unyielding. "You're going to do what I say, Joanna," he growls. "And if you don't, it won't end well for you. You understand?"

I force myself to say, "Yes," even if what I truly want to do is spit in his eye.

I scan the room quickly, noting the heavy door, the two front windows, and an exit in the back. I take a deep breath and try to calm myself down.

Thankfully, Sawyer feels the need to recount his daring escapade to the others. The men sit around a table, drinking whiskey, and some of them already appear to be drunk. Sawyer loves the sound of his own voice and goes on about how I fought him, but he prevailed.

I need to think fast and act faster while they're distracted. Panicking will do me no good. My mind races as I search for any way out, any opportunity to escape. One wrong move, and they'll know I'm trying to run, but if I wait too long, I might not get the chance. I won't be able to do anything until my legs are free, at least.

I glance at the fire poker lying within reach by the hearth. It's the only weapon I see, but I can't get to it yet—not with my arms still bound. I might be able to play along, make Sawyer think I'm willing, let him think he has control long enough for him to untie me, but then again, I can't fight off five men, no matter how hard I try. God, why isn't Jake here to save me?

Looking up at Sawyer, I force my eyes to soften, and plastering a smile on my lips. "Sawyer?" I purr, my stomach roiling. "You're right, you know." My voice drips with feigned admiration. "We'd be better together, wouldn't we?"

He pauses, his eyes narrowing like he's trying to figure out what game I'm playing. I relax, just a little, to give him the space to think I'm giving in.

"You know," I continue, making sure my tone stays light and flirtatious, "maybe I was wrong to fight you before. You're clearly in control here." I hate the way the lies feel on my tongue, but this isn't surrender—this is survival.

He steps closer, his grin widening as he watches me, surprised by my sudden change in demeanor. "You finally getting it, sweetheart?"

I nod slowly, keeping my eyes locked on his, like I'm truly considering what he's saying. "Maybe I was just too stubborn before. You're so strong, and I can see that now that you've manhandled me."

He's too drunk to notice that my words are carefully chosen, each one meant to stroke his ego. He stumbles forward and drops down on the bed next to me. I have to fight the urge to vomit when his hand comes up to caress my cheek. Every instinct in me screams to fight, to knee him in the groin, but I force myself to stay still, pretending to like it. The other men laugh, their voices low and brutish, like a pack of wild animals. It takes all of my strength not to let the revulsion show on my face, to keep up the pretense that I'm not repulsed, that I'm charmed, when every part of me wants to tear away from him.

"You've got that right, little darlin'," he mutters, leaning in a little too close, his stale whisky breath hitting my face. "Now that's better. You like me. I can tell. Maybe you'll finally start listening."

I tilt my head, pretending to be shy, my voice breathy. "I think we could have something great, Mr. Sawyer. Something really special."

He grins, showing his sharp canines. "You know what, Joanna? That's the first time you've ever said anything halfway sensible." Sawyer reaches into his pocket and pulls out a pocketknife, flipping it open. My initial reaction is to jerk away, but I have to pretend to trust him.

Keeping his glazed-over gaze on me, Sawyer cuts through the ropes binding my arms. The drunkard is both stupid and greedy, and he's convinced he has me exactly where he wants me. I have to keep him thinking I'm submissive even though every part of me is screaming to run.

"Now you're gonna learn what it means to be mine." His speech is so slurred, I can hardly understand him.

As he cuts the ropes around my ankles, I smile coyly, keeping my eyes locked on his, and letting my voice drip with honey. "Chase, you're not really going to make me your bride in front of all your friends, are you? It's not exactly the kind of thing a man like you does in front of his buddies, is it?"

He pauses, his eyes moving to the other men. "Get out," he snaps at the others.

One of them just laughs. "Hell no, Chase. We came here for a show."

Another one chimes in, grinning wide and toothless. "Yeah, we're not leaving until we all get a piece of her, too. You promised we could all have a turn."

"I don't think she'd mind," a third man says, stepping closer. "In fact, I think she's ready for it."

I can't get enough air in my lungs. Everything around me spins, and my stomach is lodged in my throat. Did I take the wrong course? The thought of one of these men touching me makes me realize I'd rather die than have their hands on me.

The ropes are gone, but that doesn't mean I'm free. There are too many of them. They're stronger than me, and I can't outrun or outfight them. Every idea I have comes up short. I don't even remember how I thought I was going to escape. I'm outnumbered, out of options, and there's nowhere to run.

I realize I might never see Jake again, and my heart sinks. How did everything go so wrong so fast?

16

A PLAN

Moonlight shines over the ranch as we finish up with the cattle. My muscles ache, but it's a familiar kind of exhaustion, the kind I've learned to live with. Andy, Jim, and Ed have already split off, heading home for the night, and I'm left standing by the corral, staring toward the house, my pack on my shoulder and the rifle I always keep with me leaning against a nearby tree.

Joanna's still not back. She went out hours ago to visit with the other women. I hope she's enjoying herself, but I miss her. I glance at the horizon, then back at the house. It's dark. She should be here by now. I clench my jaw, restless, the knot in my stomach tightening.

Moving on autopilot, I grab my gun and untie Ginger, my mind running in circles. I swing into the saddle and start toward Andy and Kathleen's house. Maybe Joanna just lost track of time, but as I ride, something doesn't sit right.

When I reach Andy's place, stars dotting the sky above me, I dismount and tie Ginger to the porch post. Impatience begins to creep in. I pound on the door, shuffling my feet as I wait for someone to answer.

Kathleen opens the door, her warm smile fading as she takes in my expression. "Jake," she says softly. "What's got you out this way?"

I try to keep my voice calm, but it cracks anyway. "Joanna. Please tell me she's still here."

Her smile fades, and her brow furrows as she searches my face. "She was here, yes, but she left hours ago. She hasn't made it home yet?"

"No, she's not. She didn't say anything about stopping anywhere else before coming home?"

Kathleen shakes her head, her eyes filled with concern. "No, she didn't mention anything. She left earlier than Laurel and Constance. She said she was heading home. She seemed excited to see you after a long day."

I hear footsteps from inside the house, and then Andy appears behind Kathleen. He must've overheard the conversation. His voice is firm, his gaze serious. "If she's not back yet, we need to go look for her."

I nod, too worried to say anything. Turning around, I scan the path toward home, my gut in a tight knot. *Where are you, Joanna?*

Andy and I ride out in the direction she would've gone, the night settling in around us. We stare into the darkness, looking for anything that might tell us where she went. I see no tracks, no signs of her at all, just land stretching out ahead of us, quiet and still.

I keep my eyes on the ground, watching for anything unusual, anything that doesn't belong. Every second that passes feels like an hour. My mind keeps drifting to the worst-case scenarios. What if she was attacked by a wild animal, something that could've caught her off guard?

We're in the middle of a cove of trees when I spot something white on the ground, partially hidden in the brush. I pull my reins hard, bringing my horse to a stop. Andy does the same, his eyes narrowing as he dismounts.

I ride closer, and as I get a better look, the sight makes my stomach drop. It's a small, torn bag, the same bag Joanna had when she left to visit with the wives. I lean down and see bread scattered around the ground, some of it crushed. The bag must've been torn in a struggle.

I dismount and crouch beside it, the knot in my chest tightening with every second. Andy steps closer, squatting down next to me. He doesn't say anything at first, but I can see it in his eyes. He's thinking the same thing I am. This is where she was when something happened—but what?

"Son of a bitch," Andy mutters, standing up straight. "Chase Sawyer."

"What?" I don't understand what he means.

"He's been threatening her for months." He shakes his head. "Look here. Bootprints in the dirt. Two sets. Big ones. Men's boots."

I see exactly what he's talking about. Standing, a drag a hand through my hair, trying to tamp down my fear so I can think. Sawyer must've ambushed her, taken her while she was walking home. I can feel the rage brewing within me as I spot the wagon tracks in the dirt.

I scan the area, looking for hoofprints in the dirt, but I see something else instead. "Andy, look," I say, pointing to the tracks. "She was taken in a wagon."

"Must've been hours ago. No tellin' how far they got." He takes a deep breath in through his nose, and it's clear he's just as terrified as I am.

"We need to get Ed, Jim, and the dogs." I move toward my horse. "Quick."

Andy remounts as well. "I'll go get the fellas," he says. "You head back to get the dogs. We'll meet here."

I give a quick nod, urging my horse into motion. The ranch house is a distant silhouette against the dark sky, still quiet with no lights. I try to push the thought of the empty home from my mind and focus on the task at hand, one thing at a time, praying we find her before it's too late.

Minutes later, the four of us are mounted and ready. The dogs pick up on the urgency in our movements, sensing something's wrong. We head out into the hills, the dogs leading the way, their noses to the ground. The wagon wheels cut deep grooves in the dirt that tell us where they've gone. The dogs keep their noses close to the ground, their ears pricked, moving ahead of us.

The night stretches on, the stars overhead barely visible through thickening clouds. My muscles ache from the ride, but I don't stop. Not even when my thoughts spiral into darker places, imagining what Sawyer might be doing to her, what he's already done. Every minute feels like an eternity.

It's the middle of the night when we finally find ourselves deep in the hills, and that's when we see a cabin. It's a small, weathered building nestled in the trees, smoke rising from the chimney.

"Stay quiet," I whisper, looking at the others. We dismount, the dogs remaining close.

Ed motions to the horses closer to the wagon. A few are tied up, with two still hitched. "Sawyer's here. That's his horse hitched to the wagon."

Hot anger coils inside me, but we need to move carefully. We can't rush in.

Andy and I exchange a look and a nod. We can't just charge in blindly. We need a plan.

Making our way through the dense underbrush, the cabin still in view at the edge of the clearing, we tie the horses a safe distance away. All of us need to stay hidden and quiet. We give the dogs a command to stay close to the horses. Tails twitch in anticipation, but all four of them obey the commands. The last thing we need is for them to alert the men inside that there's trouble brewing.

After a brief, whispered discussion, the four of us move as a unit, crawling through the tall grass and brush toward the cabin. We're close now, close enough to make out the faint sound of voices from inside. They're talking, but I can't hear what they're saying.

We find a patch of bushes not far from the cabin, low enough to stay out of sight but close enough to see the front door. "We need to get them out of there without giving them time to react." I scan the cabin, looking for an answer I cannot find.

The roof is low, the windows small, but if Sawyer's inside, he'll have a clear line of sight to the door. Trying to enter through there would be too obvious, too easy for them to shoot us.

"Have you got a plan?" Andy asks.

Everything comes into place at once as I study the cabin. "I do, but we'll have to be careful not to harm Joanna. She's in there. I can feel it." I explain to them precisely what I plan to do.

When I'm done, Ed says, "It could work."

With a nod, I say, "We wait for them to show themselves. The second they do, we shoot to kill."

17

RUN

Sawyer's face is too close, his rancid breath hot against my skin. His body looms over me, blocking any escape route, and I can feel the tension in his every movement. His hands hover over me, ready to grab, to control, and to take. My pulse pounds in my ears, and every nerve in my body screams at me to move, but I have nowhere to go. I can't breathe, can't think beyond the terror of what's about to happen.

"If you're filled up with my child, Joanna," he says, his tone low and menacing, "then you'll have to marry me. Can't have no bastard runnin' around. You're gonna stay with me, and you're gonna make sure that kid has a father."

He chuckles low, next to my ear, his breath brushing my neck, hot and revolting, and I flinch, trying to think of some way to get away from him—away from here.

"I'll make sure you're taken care of," he continues. "We'll have a home. You'll see."

I want to scream. I want to push him away, to kick him in the face with everything I have, but I know it won't work. There are five of them. I'm outnumbered, physically weaker, and the terror makes my body feel like it's made of stone, unable to move.

Outside, a loud gunshot cracks through the air, followed by the sharp sound of wood splintering. Pieces of the roof fall to the floor with a scattering clatter, and I flinch again. Sawyer stumbles back, his hand jerking away from me as his gaze snaps to the door.

"What the hell?" he mutters, looking toward the window as if trying to figure out what just happened.

I'm betting it's someone else Sawyer's pissed off, someone with a score to settle, but it doesn't matter. This is my chance to escape.

Sawyer's men are already reacting to the gunfire. "Get down!" one of them yells, diving behind the table, rifle raised.

"Who the hell is shooting at us?" another spits, pressing against the wall, his voice harsh with adrenaline.

I hold my breath, my muscles stiff with fear. The gunshots ring in my ears, and every second feels like it drags on. The men glance at each other, their eyes darting toward the door and windows. No one moves. Sawyer speaks quickly to his men, but I can't catch his words; I'm too distracted by the idea of running away. Everyone in the room is waiting, like the next shot could come any second.

This is my chance. I have to get up, to run, but if I make a sound or move too quickly, they'll catch me, and I won't survive the next step. But if I wait any longer, Sawyer and his men won't be distracted, and I'll never get another opportunity.

I just have to make sure I'm not running straight into the arms of another group of evil men.

My hands tremble as I push myself up from the bed, careful not to make a sound. I glance toward the back door. I have to be quick.

The sharp crack of another gunshot rings out, slamming into the roof with a shudder that sends pieces of wood falling to the floor. Dust swirls in the air, and the men react instantly, their eyes snapping toward the ceiling in fury. "Damnit!" Sawyer roars, slamming his fist against the table. The room erupts in chaos, voices rising in anger as the gunfire continues to shatter the silence.

In the confusion, I take my chance. Crouching low, I press my back against the wall. The men are too distracted by the noise and the danger outside to notice me moving. They're drunk and scrambling for their weapons.

I slip toward the door. Their voices grow louder as they argue, giving me the cover I need. My fingers brush the handle. The men are still distracted. It's now or never.

I twist the handle, pushing the door open just enough to slip through. I don't hesitate. I'm already moving my legs, racing toward the trees, praying they won't see me, praying this is my chance to get away. I don't look back.

Running blindly, I tear away from the cabin. The night is filled with the distant pop of gunfire. My pulse thunders in my ears, and my skin crawls with fear, but I push it down. Every inch feels like a battle. If they find me now, they'll definitely kill me.

I slip into the dark woods, my heart beating so hard it feels like it might burst from my chest. The world around me is a blur of shadows, trees looming over me, branches crashing into my face, but I don't stop to take in the surroundings. The only thing I can focus on is getting as far away from that cabin as possible.

Gunfire continues to echo behind me, sharp cracks cutting through the night air, and each one makes my blood run cold. I push myself faster, stumbling over roots and rocks, the uneven ground slowing me down, but not enough to make me stop. My lungs burn, my legs scream, but I keep going. I *have* to keep going.

I don't dare look back. Thinking about what I've just escaped only drives me forward. Branches snap underfoot, the underbrush tearing at my skin. As long as my legs continue to work, I'll ignore the pain and push on.

The woods seem endless, the night swallowing me whole, but I keep moving, putting more distance between myself and that cabin. Between myself and the men who would drag me back and assault me without a second thought. All that matters is getting back to Jake. I can't stop until I'm home.

18

FIND HER

The loud crack of my rifle echoes across the clearing as I fire at the roof of the cabin, and almost immediately, a hail of bullets comes back from inside the cabin. The windows explode, glass raining down in jagged shards, but none of the shots come close to hitting us. I drop lower behind the bushes, firing again, listening to the splintering wood and the rattle of broken glass as the men inside the cabin return fire.

They're firing blindly, but at first, none of them ventures outside. They're staying put, huddled inside, waiting for us to reveal our positions. We change up our targets, trying to confuse them. I don't know if we'll be able to get them to come out, or if I'll have to go in there and get Joanna, but I'll save her—or die trying.

One of Sawyer's men foolishly sticks his head out the broken window, trying to get a shot at whoever's firing at them. Andy doesn't hesitate. His shot rings out, hitting the man in the side of the head. He slumps where he is, hanging halfway out the window.

A large brute growls behind the dead man and rushes to the door. He drunkenly stumbles out onto the porch, gun raised in one hand, the other hand flailing to keep his balance. "You bastards killed my brother! You ain't gonna walk away from this!" His words are slurred but full of menace. Jim, who's taken a position at the front of the house behind a large tree, fires. From where I'm kneeling in the bushes on the side of the house, I don't get a clear view of where the shot lands, but the man jerks back and collapses onto the porch with a heavy thud.

Across the lawn, Ed motions for us to stay put before darting toward the cabin. He takes a shot, and a moment later, he's back, hurrying toward me, dropping behind the bushes.

"Did you get anybody?" I ask.

"Yeah. I hit one," Ed says. "Sawyer's still in there and one other man."

"Is Joanna all right?" I whisper.

"I didn't see her. She's probably hiding somewhere so she doesn't get hit."

We have three men down, with Sawyer and one other man still inside. I can't waste any more time. I need them out of that cabin—now.

I have three flashlights in my pack. Sawyer and his men have never seen anything like them, and if I shine them through the windows, move the beams fast, dart them from one spot to the next, Sawyer will have no choice but to notice. It'll distract them long enough for the others to take them out, but using the flashlights means blowing my cover.

When Ed, Andy, and Jim see the flashlights, they'll start asking questions I'm not ready to answer. They'll wonder why I've got gear they don't recognize, but Joanna's still in there, and I'm not about to let anything stop me now.

My mind is made up. I have to do what needs to be done. "I'm going to distract them. You wait until they're confused, and then take them out."

Ed nods and motions to Jim and Andy. The three of them have worked together long enough to know what he means without words.

With a deep breath, I pull the flashlights from my bag, flick them on, and aim them at the windows, moving them around wildly. Gasps from my friends barely register as the beams cut through the dark, fast and erratic. It's enough to make them second-guess what they're seeing. They won't know what to make of it.

It doesn't take long before one of the men appears in the broken window, his gun already raised, aiming out into the night. I keep the flashlight on him, the beam darting fast enough to throw off his aim. He doesn't have time to react. Andy's shot rings out, and the man jerks as the bullet hits, dropping him before he can even return fire.

That leaves Sawyer. I know he's still in there. I don't stop moving the flashlights. I keep them dancing across the windows, quick and wild.

Creeping closer, I stay low until I'm within range. The bastard's barely visible behind the broken window, his gun raised. I position all three flashlights, aiming them right at his face, the beams flickering and darting. For a split second, his eyes widen, caught in the light. That's all it takes. One of the ranch hands behind me shoots, and Sawyer drops, his gun clattering to the floor.

My only regret is that I couldn't kill the asshole myself.

Adrenaline pumps through my veins as the sound of Sawyer's body hitting the ground rings in my ears. My heart's still pounding, the last shot echoing in my skull. I can't afford to get caught up in what just happened. I'm usually the one mending gunshots, not helping make them. But I've got to find Joanna.

"Move!" I shout, already heading for the cabin door, the others following close behind. Shoving my flashlights into my pockets, I push the door open. The air inside is suffocating with gun smoke and the stench of blood. The bodies of Sawyer's men lie scattered around the floor, but there's no sign of Joanna.

I move through the room quickly, checking under tables, sliding furniture aside, trying to think of any place where someone could hide. Nothing. There's no trace of her anywhere. "Joanna?" I shout, but the cabin is only one room—there aren't many places to hide.

Turning around, I search the other men's eyes for answers.

"Where the hell is she?" Jim mutters, his voice tight with frustration. "The bed has ropes lyin' on it. She had to be here."

"The back door's open," Ed says, pointing across the room. The door's ajar, barely noticeable in the chaos. I don't waste any time.

"She's very clever," I say. "She probably ran out the back after the first shot."

The thought that she might have slipped out and made a run for it is enough to make my stomach tighten. I can't imagine how terrified she must've been, but she still had the gumption to get out. I only hope she's all right, and we can find her quickly.

"We'll have to move fast," I tell them. "She can't be far."

We step outside, and I look around. It's dark out here, and this isn't a place any of us are familiar with. If she's not right outside, she must not know it's us. She might've decided to run home—if she can find her way.

I wave one of my flashlights around, but I don't see any sign of her.

"Where the hell did you get those funny lights, Jake?" Andy asks next to me.

I hesitate for a moment, but there's no time for this conversation anyway. I won't lie. I'll just keep it vague for now.

"I brought them from home," I say simply, locking eyes with him. "I'll explain more later, but right now, we need to find her."

They all glance at each other, confusion clear on their faces, but they don't ask any more questions. There's no time for that.

"Let's get the horses and the dogs." Ed's voice is sharp with urgency.

I hand a flashlight to Andy and one to Ed, keeping the last for myself. We move toward the trees, the flashlights cutting through the dark. The dogs are waiting, ready to find Joanna. Their noses will be of more use to us than anything else, including the flashlights.

With the cabin behind us, the smell of death still lingering in the air, there's no time for reflection. We mount our horses quickly, the animals restless, sensing the urgency of the next part of our mission. I nudge Ginger forward, keeping a tight grip on the reins as the flashlight bobs in my hand. The light cuts through the trees, moving over branches and uneven ground as we push deeper into the woods.

The dogs move ahead, their noses working the air. They know

what they're doing. They'll pick up her scent, and once they do, we'll have a trail to follow.

"She went north toward home!" Ed calls, his flashlight bouncing through the tree line. He holds it like he's not sure he can trust it, but he's using it correctly, and that's all that matters. "We'll catch up to her in no time."

The dogs keep moving, leading us deeper into the woods, and though I know we're getting closer, there's still no sign of her.

We ride on, knowing the next few hours are critical. She could be injured. She could've been hurt by Sawyer before she ran, and now she's exposed to the dangers of the wild out here. Every second counts.

I push Ginger faster, my eyes darting through the dark. She's out here somewhere, and I won't stop until I find her.

19

I NEED YOU

I've been running in a curved path for hours so that Sawyer can't track me. The dark seemed endless, and now, with the first light creeping through the trees, I can barely tell how far I've gone. My legs ache, my feet are raw inside my boots, and my lungs burn, but I can't stop.

Every sound makes me flinch. Branches snapping, a rustling in the distance. There are animals out here that could tear me apart, and I have a feeling someone is following me. Visions of Chase leaping from behind a tree and snatching me give me the energy to keep moving despite my exhaustion.

The forest is quieter now, the wind barely moving through the leaves. The pale yellow light of dawn starts to brighten the sky, so at least now I can see where I'm going.

Despite better vision, tiredness makes me stumble over a root and nearly fall, catching myself just in time. I'm really not sure which direction home is. I know I need to head south, but I've never been this deep in the woods before, and it's easy to get turned around.

A twig snaps behind me, and it's clear something is there. I duck behind a tree and hold my breath. Someone or something tramples through the leaves, not even trying to be quiet. My heart leaps in my chest, and I go still, every muscle tensed, as I wait for a monster to emerge. Should I stay here, cowering behind this tree, or run?

Fear surges through my body, and I find myself unable to move. I squeeze my eyes closed as the footsteps get closer.

And then I hear a bark.

"Margot?" I whisper, unable to believe it's true. Peeking around the tree, I squint into the dim light, looking for my best friend.

She's there, bounding through the underbrush, tail wagging furiously. I drop to my knees, laughing and crying at the same time as she rushes into my arms.

"Margot! What are you doing out here, you silly ol' girl?" I ask. "You found me!"

She licks my face and yips, and I hold on to her like she's a lifeline —which she is. A moment later, more rustling alerts me to more company. Huck emerges, followed by Lady, then Ace, all of them looking a little worse for wear but determined. They surround me, all of them wanting pets and to be assured they've done their job.

"You're actually here!" I stroke each of their heads, falling back onto my bottom, tears slipping from my eyes. "You're here."

A rumble in the distance quickly grows louder, and I recognize approaching hoofbeats. I stand and hold my breath, praying to see the face I've been dreaming of throughout my entire ordeal.

Jake appears, leading Ginger through the underbrush, with Ed, Andy, and Jim behind him.

When Jake's eyes meet mine, he dismounts in one fluid motion. I run to him. He gathers me up, pulling me against his chest. I bury my face into his shoulder, too relieved to speak.

"Joanna," he whispers, kissing the top of my head. "Thank God we found you. Are you hurt?"

"I'm not hurt. I didn't know it was you following me," I say, my voice shaking. "I thought it was Sawyer."

He pulls back just enough to look me in the eye, his hand cradling my face, and I can see the fire in his gaze. "No one's ever going to hurt you again. I promise."

The others have dismounted now, and they are standing nearby, watching with that mix of concern and relief. "We're glad you're all right, Joanna," Ed says.

"We've been tracking you for hours," Andy adds. "You sure did take a windy path."

Jim drags a hand through his hair. "We took out Sawyer and his men. They're all dead."

My eyes widen, and my mouth drops open. "He's dead?" I can hardly believe it. A burst of happiness blooms in my chest that I don't want to claim, but now he can't hurt me or any other woman ever again. He's not going to show up unannounced anymore. He won't bully, insult, or threaten me. He can't touch me again. I don't have to fear him anymore.

"You're safe now, darling," Jake says, smoothing a hand across my cheek. "Forever."

All I can say is, "Thank you." I release Jake so that I can hug each of my ranch hands, tears of joy still streaming down my cheeks.

"I bet you're hungry." Jake pulls a strip of jerky from his pack and hands it to me. "And thirsty." He also hands me a canteen.

My stomach growls as I greedily take the food. "Thank you." I take a long drink from the canteen and graciously accept an apple as well.

"Let's let the horses rest a spell," Ed suggests. The ranch hands lead them over to a shady spot, giving Jake and me a moment alone. We sink down beneath the branches of a large tree with the dogs curled around us, keeping watch. I rest my head against Jake's shoulder and close my eyes, letting myself calm. The worry that's gnawed at me all night starts to ease. It's still early, and there's a long ride ahead of us, but for the first time since Chase grabbed me and threw me in his wagon, I feel safe.

"Rest for a bit." Jake kisses my forehead, his arm wrapped around my shoulders tight. "Then, we'll head back home."

All I can do is nod and finish eating, thankful to be alive and back with my family.

The ride home is slow, the sound of the horses' hooves breaking the quiet of the morning. Everything that happened is still a fresh, raw wound, but now that I'm back with Jake, it feels like I can finally relax. I sit in front of him on Ginger, glad to have his protective arms wrapped around me.

The moment the familiar landscape of my ranch comes into sight, I feel even more tension melt from my shoulders. Jake chuckles gently and kisses my cheek. "Home, sweet home."

As we reach the fork where Andy, Jim, and Ed turn off toward their houses, Jake slows the horse and pulls to a stop. I look at each of them, my voice soft but sincere. "Thank you again... for finding me, and for getting rid of Chase Sawyer. I appreciate you three more than you could ever know."

They tip their hats to me, and Ed gives me a smile. "You don't need to say anything," he replies. "We all did what needed to be done."

Andy nods. "We're just glad you're safe." He urges his horse forward, heading down the path to his wife and kids.

"Should've shot that yellow bellied shitheel the moment I met him," Jim mutters before turning and following the others.

Jake and I watch as the others ride off, the quiet settling in as they disappear down the road. The moment hangs there for a beat before Jake gently nudges Ginger forward. "Come on. We're almost home."

The rest of the ride is quick. More tears spill over when my little home comes into view. For a spell, I didn't know if I'd ever see it again.

Jake dismounts and helps me down and then leads Ginger toward the barn. I head inside, the dogs trailing me. I'm still a little unsteady, but grateful to be back.

Once inside, I sit down at the kitchen table, exhausted. A few moments later, Jake walks through the door, his gaze meeting mine as he steps inside. "Ginger's happy for a bite to eat," he says. A glance at the dogs, who are scarfing down everything in their bowls, has him chuckling. "She's not the only one."

I laugh, but I can't speak at the moment.

Dropping his bag down on the floor, he turns to me. "How about a bath?"

I nod. He takes my hand and leads me to my room, where the tub sits by the hearth. I lie on the bed nearby, and as Jake heads out to get the water, I close my eyes for just a moment. I'm actually here—in my own bed.

When he finishes filling the bath, Jake sets a clean towel on the stool beside the tub. His eyes roam over me as if he isn't sure I'm actually here either. He takes a shuddering breath and a few steps in my direction.

I sit up, reaching for his hand. "I don't know what I would've done if I didn't have you," I whisper, my voice cracking. "You saved me."

His eyes soften, and he sits down next to me, brushing a strand of hair from my face. "You don't have to thank me," he says. "I'll always find you. Always."

I swallow the lump in my throat, hugging him tight. He helps me out of my filthy clothes, and I step into the tub, the hot water enveloping me like a cocoon. The aches start to fade, but the gratitude in my heart only grows.

He kneels down next to me and lathers up a cloth with a bar of soap, washing my back. I close my eyes and relish the feel of him. With a deep breath, I say, "I didn't realize how much I needed someone like you."

It takes him a moment to speak, and when he does, I can hear the lump in his throat. "You mean everything to me, Joanna."

The words that slip from my lips are not frightening. They are a truth that I've known for a while but just didn't acknowledge. "I love you, Jake."

He runs a hand along my cheek. "I love you, too, Joanna, and I'll keep you safe." He swipes a tear away from my cheek, and when I lean toward him, his lips meet mine in a soft, warm kiss.

Jake lathers shampoo in his hands and massages it into my hair, the pressure of his fingers making my scalp tingle. He uses the pitcher to rinse it out, and I let out a soft sigh. It feels so good to have him take care of me like this.

He runs the cloth over my skin, his touch gentle. He works his way down my neck and arms, never rushing. When he reaches my breasts, I can't help the moan that slips from my lips as a shiver of pleasure rushes through me.

Jake moves the cloth over my belly, sending little sparks of warmth through my skin. He works his way down my legs, then back up my thighs, his touch lingering just enough to make my heart race. He scrubs every inch carefully, then leans down to kiss my forehead, a sweet, affectionate gesture. I close my eyes, savoring every moment of his attention, feeling more cherished than I ever have before.

He lathers his hands with soap, his gaze never leaving mine, and lowers his hand into the water. With slow, delicious strokes, he cleans my most delicate parts, his touch tender and thorough. Every movement ignites something inside me, each sensation deeper and more intense than the last.

I moan and lean forward, my head and arms resting on the side of the tub, giving him more space to tease me. He circles with one finger and pushes two other fingers inside, causing my hips to buck in pleasure. "Jake, that feels so good."

He kisses me again, sliding his fingers back in, then out—faster and faster until I'm gasping and the water splashes out of the tub. "Jake, don't stop!" I moan.

A wave of release rumbles through me, my body relaxing as all the tension melts away. I lay back in the warm water, breathing deeply as I let my body go limp, feeling the calm wash over me. Jake reaches over and takes my hand, kissing it lightly.

"Thank you," I whisper.

He nods, releasing my hand, and stands. Without a word, he holds out the towel. I step out of the tub, and he wraps me up in it.

Jake dries me off quickly, then he pulls me close, and we kiss, the heat between us rising with every second. The towel drops, and he lifts me into his arms, swinging me around to the bed, and gently lays me down, his gaze never leaving mine.

I frantically pull his shirt off and undo his belt while he kisses a trail down my neck.

"You're the most beautiful woman I've ever seen," he says, finding a breast with his lips.

"Jake, please take me," I whisper.

He stands and finishes undressing, revealing every plane of his perfectly sculpted body to me, and is positioned between my thighs within seconds.

"I need you," I beg.

Jake pushes inside of me, filling me completely. He continues to stroke the perfect spot, each movement building the pressure until we both fall over the edge. We lock eyes, and he kisses me softly, murmuring about how much he loves me, how he'll never let me go again.

The rhythm of his breathing and the warmth of his body against mine are a safe haven, and before long, I drift off, falling asleep in his arms.

20

DRINKING WATER

A few days pass, and all I can think about is how lucky I am that Joanna is back safe and sound. I can hardly stand to let her out of my sight. But life on the ranch goes on, and we work in harmony, as we did before the nightmare of her kidnapping. A few times, the fellas have asked about the flashlights, but so far, I've managed to blow them off. They think they're odd—but no one suspects I'm from the future.

The sun's barely up when I step out onto the porch, the air still cool before the sun rises, but the heat of the day is coming. Joanna's already by the water trough, scrubbing out the feed buckets. She looks up and flashes me a smile.

We're in the middle of our daily chores when I hear hooves approaching fast, kicking up dust behind them. I turn just in time to see Kathleen on Andy's mare, galloping up to us. She pulls up short, her eyes filled with terror, her breath ragged.

"Jake! Joanna! It's Andy—he and the kids are sick. Real bad. You gotta come quick." Her tone is frantic as she tries to steady the horse that's mirroring her nervous energy.

My stomach drops. "Sick how?"

She shakes her head, not wasting any time on explanations. "Fever, chills. Can't hardly stand up. You gotta help us."

I exchange a glance with Joanna. Her lips press into a thin line, and she gives a sharp nod. "Get Ginger and Chaco ready."

I race to the barn, saddle both horses, and lead them back to Joanna. We ride hard, the horses moving at a swift trot. I'm already planning ahead and trying to think of supplies we might need that aren't in my pack. We'll need plenty of boiled water, blankets, herbs that might help with fever and chills.

When we reach Andy's place, Kathleen is the first to dismount, her face pale and eyes wide with worry. She rushes to the door, slamming it open. We follow her inside to the bedroom where Andy's lying in bed, drenched in sweat, his breathing shallow.

I kneel next to him, pressing my hand to his forehead. He's burning up. "Andy, can you hear me?" His eyes open for a second, then close again, and I don't like the look of him. He's far too weak.

Kathleen stands at the foot of the bed, wringing her shaking hands. "I... I don't know what to do. I've been trying to get water into them, but it's like they can't even swallow. They ain't got enough strength."

I step into the children's bedroom, and they all look just as sick. The fever is obvious, their faces flushed and slick with sweat. One is barely moving, her chest rising and falling with shallow breaths. They're all so still with their eyes half-closed, too weak to respond when I approach. Their skin is hot to the touch, and I can see the tremor in their bodies, the way they shiver despite the warmth in the room. It's the same signs: fever, dehydration, and weakness, and it's clear this is much worse than any common cold or flu. I feel the urgency in my gut, knowing we don't have much time.

I meet Joanna's eyes. We both know there's no doctor around here to help. We'll have to make do with what we've got. The heat of the afternoon sun pours through the windows, and it feels like the walls are closing in.

"We'll do what we can," I say. "Let's get them cooled down and keep them hydrated with water that's been boiled."

Joanna sets to work immediately, sponging Andy's face with cool water while I start feeding his kids small sips of broth Kathleen made. It's slow going. They can barely drink, and their hands are too weak to hold the cup. I explain to Kathleen in terms I hope she can understand. "Don't drink anything that hasn't been boiled. That's what's causing this—bad water. We've got to get enough fluids in them to replace the bad fluid with clean."

She nods, swiping at tears that trail down her cheeks as she helps her youngest drink some broth.

We stay for a few hours, getting as much fluids into the children and Andy as we can. I don't have enough antibiotics in my bag to help all of them, but since the youngest seems to be suffering the most, I manage to grind some up while Kathleen and Joanna aren't looking and slip it into the broth.

By early evening, they all seem to be doing better, and Kathleen understands the importance of continuing to hydrate them. But something has been weighing on my mind since we arrived. All three of the ranch hands' homes have wells that are fed from the same source. "Let's check on Jim and Ed," I whisper to Joanna. "They might be sick, too."

Joanna nods, and we saddle up. When we reach Jim's place, it's more of the same. Jim and his wife are both lying in bed, their faces red and slick with sweat. Their kids are in the same shape, their bodies trembling despite the warmth in the room. Fluids are passing right through them, as evidenced by the stack of dirty laundry tossed in the corner.

"God, what's happening?" Joanna whispers, her voice thick with worry.

I can explain it, but now is not the time. "We'll keep 'em drinking water." I force a smile. "We'll get them through it."

She gives me a confident nod, but this is going to be trickier since every member of the household is sick, so no one can help. We stay for a few hours, getting them hydrated with chicken broth Joanna heats up and boiled water.

Eventually, we have to head out to Ed's place. By now, the sky's starting to dim, and I'm feeling the strain in my body and my heart. We're running on fumes, but we have no choice but to keep going.

At the third house, Ed and his wife are barely able to sit up, their children lying motionless in their beds.

Hours pass in a blur of boiling water and applying cool cloths. There's just so many mouths to fill and only the two of us to do so. We press on, encouraging the children to drink even when their little heads lull to the side with exhaustion.

As night falls, I look at Joanna. The glow has left her eyes, and her hands are shaking from working nonstop. We haven't eaten all day, and if we don't take a break soon, we'll end up sick ourselves. Not from this—thank goodness—but worn down, nevertheless.

The evening stretches on, and the work never stops. We move from one house to the other, boiling water, wiping brows, and coaxing sips from parched lips. It's a blur of exhaustion and sickness. We pause only long enough to take a few bites of jerky and barely sip water ourselves. I can see how exhausted Joanna is, and I know we've done about all we can do.

The moon is high in the sky when I finish spoon feeding Ed's youngest a cup of broth. "Joanna, let's head back to the house." My voice is hoarse from hours of talking, soothing, and urging them to drink.

She nods, her eyes half closed from fatigue. Silently, we mount up again, but I know she's thinking the same thing I am. Will our friends make it through the night?

The ride back to the house is quiet… too quiet. This should have been a peaceful day, and we should be asleep in our bed now, but we both feel the dread creeping in.

Joanna and I lead the horses into the barn and care for them before heading inside. She goes straight to the washbasin to rinse off, but I stand in the kitchen for a moment, staring out the window, my mind racing.

The symptoms are fever, chills, dehydration, weakness, glassy eyes, arrhythmia, and vomiting. My years of training to become an EMT tell me exactly what the illness is: cholera.

I've known it since the first moment I looked at Andy. The realization had hit me like a slap in the face. The pieces fell into place: the way the family members are so weak, the way they can hardly keep anything down, how they're barely able to stay conscious. It's all there, in the symptoms, in the way their bodies are shutting down.

This is a disease none of them here will know how to treat. It's a disease none of them in 1870s New Mexico will be familiar with, and it can kill in a matter of hours if it's left unchecked.

I run a hand through my hair, pacing, the weight of the world resting on my shoulders. I'm the only one who knows what this is, and I'm the only one who might have any chance at stopping it from killing people. All I've got are my instincts, and the knowledge from the world I came from—a world where cholera isn't a death sentence.

Joanna finishes washing up and sits at the table, her face pale. She looks up at me as I stop pacing, a furrow in her brow. "What's going on, Jake?" Her voice is filled with concern. She knows me well enough to recognize when I'm thinking too hard and when something's got me rattled.

I step over to her. "They've got cholera." My voice is low but firm. "The fever, the cramps, the dehydration—I'm certain that's what this is. It comes from dirty drinking water."

Her eyes widen, and she stands up quickly, and she reaches for me. "Cholera? How do you know?"

"I've seen it before, back where I'm from." I don't even want to think about that right now—about the century that's so different from this one. A time where we have vaccines, antibiotics, IV fluids, and all kinds of treatments they don't have here. "It's a waterborne disease. It spreads fast, and it's deadly. We have to keep treating them."

"Then that's what we'll do." Her voice is sharp, decisive. "What else can we do to help them?"

I feel a pang of guilt, knowing I have to rely on knowledge she doesn't have, knowledge from a time and place she can't even comprehend. "Like I said before, we need to keep them drinking water. That's the key. Water's the most important thing. But we also need to make a kind of solution to add to the water. We need to boil the water for a long time and then make soup with a lot of salt. That will help replace the electrolytes they're losing, help their bodies hold on to the water."

"Electrolytes?" Her eyebrows furrow.

I take a deep breath, reminding myself to be careful. "It's a fancy word for a nutrient our bodies can't live without."

"Anything else?" she asks.

I shake my head, feeling a lump form in my throat. "That's all I know to do right now, and that's truly what we've been doing all day. For now, we need to get some rest and then go back, first thing in the morning, and start all over again. We don't have much time."

"I want to help them," she says, tears in her eyes.

"I do, too, but if we are too tired to stand up, we won't be able to help anyone."

She nods reluctantly, and the two of us head off to bed for a few hours, wrapped in one another's arms.

With the first light of morning, I move to the stove and light a fire to start boiling water for the soup. All I can think about are the families out there, and I pray that everyone made it through the night.

"Jake..." Joanna's voice is groggy from sleep but firm as she looks at me, her hand resting lightly on my arm. "We can save them."

I turn to face her, and I see the trust in her eyes. The trust that I don't even feel in myself yet, but I can't let her down. I can't let any of them down.

"We have to try," I say.

Thankfully, when we check each home, everyone is still hanging on. Then, the day becomes a blur, just like the one before, as we keep working, moving from one house to the next, feeding them sips of the salty soup, wiping their fevered faces, and coaxing them to drink as much as we can. The sickness doesn't relent, but we do start to see some improvement the longer we work.

By the time night falls, we're exhausted. We're running on fumes, but neither of us says it aloud. Our bodies are sore, our minds numb from the strain, but we keep going, because they're counting on us, and they're our friends. The darkness presses in, but we don't stop. Every drop of the soup, every cool cloth on their foreheads, feels like it could make the difference. All we can do now is keep them hydrated, keep them comfortable, and pray.

21

KEEP GOING

Joanna

We ride through the quiet morning, the sun barely starting to lighten the sky. After several long, grueling days of caring for the cowhands and their families, it feels like my body's made of lead.

It's only when we near the well that Jake slows his horse, his voice breaking the silence. "Joanna, there's got to be something wrong with their well."

I glance at him, still disoriented from the long night. "What do you mean?"

Jake dismounts and drops Ginger's reins. "This disease is usually spread from human waste. If the lining of the well is compromised," he says, walking over to the well, "the water would be contaminated."

I nod, not questioning it. He leans down and looks into the well for a few moments. I stand back, watching. After a moment, he lowers the bucket. The rope scrapes against the stone, the sound echoing around us. We wait, listening to the dull thud as it sinks deeper into the water.

After a long minute, the rope goes taut. Jake starts pulling it up, slowly and carefully.

When the bucket breaks the surface, I catch a glimpse of what's inside: a bloated, lifeless rat, its fur slick with decay. It floats grotesquely, water sloshing around it. My stomach churns at the sight, and I fight the urge to vomit.

"Well, hell," I mutter. "That's what's been making everyone sick?"

Jake shakes his head. "Actually, no. The rat died from the same disease they have now. Look here." He bends down again, and I follow his pointing finger. "See that crack? Where the mortar's loose? That's the problem. The water is contaminated."

I'm quiet for a moment. I know Jake and I are the only ones who avoided illness, but I never understood how we managed to avoid it.

Jake dumps the bucket into the brush. The sickening smell lingers.

"How did we not get sick?" I ask. "Our water all comes from the same place."

"The lining of our well isn't cracked, but I always boil our water for a very long time before using it for drinking or cooking, and I drop the purification tablets in our canteens. We'll have to drain this well, clean it out properly, and fix the cracks." Jake says.

I nod. Jake's always thinking ahead, making sure everything is taken care of, even when the rest of us seem to be falling apart. I admire that about him.

The exhaustion of the past night creeps in, but there's something grounding in the way Jake handles it all. I step closer to him, knowing there's more work to do, but right now, in this quiet moment, I'm grateful for him, for the way he's always looked out for me and always kept me safe without asking for anything in return. I wrap my arms around him and kiss him soundly.

After a few moments, he pulls away. Smiling, he asks, "What was that for?"

"For being you," I say with a shrug. "I love you, Jake."

"I love you, too."

The ride from the well to the house is short, but the weariness of the past few days drags me down. Jake leads the way, his shoulders hunched under the weight of the exhaustion we both feel.

When we finally reach the house, Jake dismounts first, his boots hitting the ground with a dull thud, and then he helps me down. He leads Chaco and Ginger into the barn, where we unsaddle them in the cool shade. My legs are sore from the long ride and hours of work, but together we start the familiar tasks of caring for the horses.

"We'll wash up, get some food, and rest for a bit," Jake says.

I nod, understanding. As much as my body craves rest, the fear and sorrow of my good friends being so ill runs through my mind, but there's no time to dwell. We've got work to do.

Inside, I set to washing my hands and face, scrubbing away the grime. Our water has already been boiled, of course, and it feels good to rinse off. Jake stands at the stove, tending to a pot of coffee.

After we eat a light meal, we take a rest. I awaken a few hours later, wrapped in Jake's arms. His eyes are still heavy with tiredness. "We need to get back out there, and check on Jim and the others."

I stop what I'm doing and turn to him, already knowing what he means. "Jim and Constance aren't getting better, are they?" My words feel heavy, and I'm already dreading the answer.

Jake doesn't need to say it; I can see it in his face. "Not yet. They seem to be getting worse."

I take a deep breath. "Let's go."

We saddle up again, this time giving Chaco and Ginger a break. I'm riding Bridgit, and Jake's on Starfire.

When we arrive at Jim's house, it's worse than I expected. Jim and Constance still lie in their bed, their faces flushed, eyes glazed over with fever. The six children are still too weak to even lift their heads. They're barely conscious, their faces pale, their breath shallow. The room smells of sweat and sickness, and I can see the faint signs of dehydration on each of their faces.

Jake grabs a cup of water from the kitchen and moves to Constance's side, his hand gently pressing against her forehead. "Constance, you need to drink some water," he says softly.

She barely responds, her body too weak to even acknowledge him. Jake tries again, lifting the cup to her lips, but she can barely swallow.

I kneel beside the children, checking each of them in turn. The smallest one stirs, and his feverish skin feels like it's burning to the touch. I move to the older girl next, her eyes fluttering as she shifts slightly under the covers. She doesn't have the strength to speak, only gazes up at me with dull, tired eyes. I wipe the sweat from her forehead and offer her a sip of water, but she can barely choke it down before regurgitating it back up.

When we've given every member of Jim's family a sip of the soup we made from clean water, with extra salt, and a fresh cold compress for their faces, Jake turns back to me. "We have to keep going."

I meet his eyes and nod, though the pit in my stomach tells me we're running out of time. The others—Andy and his kids, Ed and Laurel and their children—are slowly improving. They're still weak, but their fevers are breaking. They're responsive now, taking small sips of water and broth, holding on. Somehow, Kathleen didn't get sick at all. When we asked her if she'd drank much water lately, she said she doesn't drink too much water. She prefers milk and whiskey. To think that the whiskey may have saved her life….

But Jim, Constance, and their children are not getting any better. The sickness is too far advanced for them.

We move between houses, offering broth and comfort, trying to ease their suffering. It feels like we're working in a haze, every movement mechanical as we move from one room to the next, one bed to the next, but it never feels like enough.

At Ed and Laurel's place a few hours later, their three children are still feverish, but they're awake and more alert than they were when we left. The relief in Laurel's eyes is barely perceptible, but it's there. Ed's still too weak to do much, but he's holding on, the worst of it over for him.

When we finally reach Jim and Constance's again, their children have grown even more pale, their bodies trembling with each shallow breath. Constance is barely conscious, her eyes fluttering open only to close again, her body sinking further into the fever.

"We're losing them," I whisper, not wanting to say it out loud, but it's true.

Jake doesn't answer, but I know he feels it, too. He knows that they can't fight this much longer.

We work late, doing what we can to ease their suffering, and I pray they can hold on long enough to make it through the night.

22

BEYOND THE COTTONWOODS

Jake and I ride up to Andy and Kathleen's house, tying our horses to the fence post outside. I raise my hand to knock, but the door opens before I touch it. Kathleen appears, her face lined with exhaustion but calm, and she steps aside to let us in. The family sits at the table, pale and thin, sipping broth from small bowls and nibbling pieces of bread. Andy manages to lift his face to us with a small smile, but he doesn't speak. One of the children offers a small wave before taking a sip of water.

"They're doing better," Kathleen says.

I nod. "Good. We were worried about you." I hand a pot of chicken bone broth to Kathleen. "This will help, too, but listen, Kathleen, this is very important. Remember what we told you yesterday. You cannot drink water from that well, and whatever you do, don't drink any water that hasn't been boiled first."

She nods. "Yes, of course. I remember."

Jake moves from child to child, holding a small contraption he brought from his pack. He calls it a thermometer, though I've never seen one shaped like this one before. He places it under a child's arm, then the next, and finally announces with a big smile, "Their fevers have broken."

Relief washes over me, and I let myself take a deep breath, grateful that the worst is behind them. Inside, I'm still bracing myself for what we might find elsewhere. We say our goodbyes and ride out, thankful that this family will make a full recovery.

Ed and Laurel's house is next. Their three children are sitting upright, shaky, but able to hold their heads and reach for bowls of broth. Laurel sits at the table, spoon feeding one of her little ones. Ed adjusts a blanket and hands water to a child sitting in a chair by the hearth. They are still pale, but they're alive and recovering. I use their chicken stock to make a pot of broth and heat it up for them, and Jake helps boil water. He takes their temperatures, and again, the thermometer gives us good news. We remind them not to use the well, and to boil all the water they use again.

When we see that they are strong enough to manage without us, I take a deep breath and say a quiet prayer of gratitude, and as we ride toward Jim and Constance's house, a spark of hope rises in me, thinking maybe everyone will get better.

We reach Jim and Constance's house and tie the horses to the fence post. I step up to the door and lift my hand to knock, but no one answers. After a moment, worried, we push the door open and step inside.

I call out, "Jim? Constance?" The house is silent. With a sinking feeling, we move through the sitting room and into the bedroom. Jim and Constance lie side by side on the bed, completely still, their faces pale and slack. I can hardly breathe. Jake kneels beside them, lifts Jim's wrist, then Constance's, and shakes his head. "They're gone," he says quietly.

I choke back a sob as we run to the children's bedroom, forcing myself to keep moving even though my stomach churns at what I might find. Two of the children, Chuck and Glory, lie still on their beds, already gone, and my heart overflows with grief.

"Oh, Jesus! Help us," I whisper.

One of the children, little Alice, who is only two, is asleep or unconscious, and she's having trouble breathing. Her chest is barely rising, and Jake kneels beside the child's bed, pressing on her little chest, holding her nose and blowing into her mouth again and again. I have no idea what he's doing, but he always knows what to do in these situations, so I move among the other three children. I check their breathing and try to soothe them as best I can. They are weak and trembling but alive.

Slowly, Alice's tiny chest finally rises more fully, the child drawing real breaths. "Thank God you were here, Jake. You saved Alice's life."

"We need to get them out of here as soon as possible," he says. "It's not good for them to be in this environment anymore." He doesn't have to explain to me why. "I'll go get the wagon, and we can take them to Andy and Kathleen."

I nod and help the weak children sip clean water and warm bone broth. While Jake heads home for the wagon, I cradle little Alice and sing them a lullaby my mother used to sing to me when I was sick.

When Jake returns with the wagon, he lifts the sick children one at a time from their beds into the wagon bed, where he's laid fresh straw and quilts. I carry little Alice, and he takes her so I can climb into the wagon seat, then hands her back to me. He even thought to bring her a fresh bottle of goat's milk. She drinks from the freshly cleaned bottle, although she's still quite weak. Every shallow breath she takes reminds me of her two siblings we could not save and her parents we lost.

We reach Andy's house, and Jake jumps out of the wagon and knocks. Kathleen opens the door, and he tells her that Jim and Constance are gone. She lifts her hands to her face, crying, and Andy comes up behind her. She tells him, and he pulls her close, holding her tight. I stay in the wagon, watching, unable to hear a word, but I can tell everything from how they move, how she leans into her husband, and how he holds her.

Kathleen walks over to the wagon, her eyes still brimming with tears, and reaches for Alice. I hand the baby to her, and she cradles her gently. "I'll take good care of her," she says, and I know she will.

Andy and Jake lift the other three children from the wagon,

carrying them carefully into the house, and I watch, tears streaming, knowing they'll be safe. Of course, Jake and I will be here to help as much as possible. But Kathleen is a mother, and I am not. She knows best when it comes to how to raise children.

I climb down from the wagon and go into the house to help everyone get settled. The older children look apprehensive, so I reassure them that they'll be safe and feel better soon. I can see in their eyes that they are worried about their missing family members, but I don't explain that they've passed away, not yet. It wouldn't do anyone any good.

Jake and I thank Andy and Kathleen for caring for the children and ask if they need anything before we head home to rest. Shaking her head, Kathleen says, "We're all feeling better. You've done enough. Go home and sleep."

By the time Jake and I make it home, the sun is setting, but there's no rest. The animals still need to be cared for. We move through the chores mechanically, the memory of Jim, Constance, and the two children pressing down on me. Jake stays beside me constantly, lifting what I can't, holding me when my hands shake, and letting me lean into him without question.

Night falls, and we sit on the porch, exhausted. My whole body aches with grief. I can't help but think about how still they all were, how ghostly pale.

"We'll have to tend to their bodies." Jake's voice is just a whisper.

I press my hands to my face. "I… I can't bear to do it tonight."

He nods, "We'll do it first thing in the morning."

The children who survived the illness are safe, and two of the three families are recovering, but the ones we could not save—Jim, Constance, Chuck, and Glory—I will carry their memory with me forever.

Morning comes too soon, the summer sun climbing over the horizon with a promise of nothing but stifling heat today. The light feels too bright and ordinary for what we have to do. Grief does not lift with the dawn; it takes deep root.

Andy and Kathleen stay home with all the children—Jim and

Constance's surviving four, and Ed and Laurel's children as well so they can help us, though I think they're too weak to do so. Kathleen insisted on keeping all the children together, saying the house is full but strong, that no child will be left alone today. I am grateful for it.

We wrap Jim, Constance, Chuck, and Glory in clean sheets and take them out to the low hill beyond the cottonwoods. It's quiet here, the land wide and bare, the sky stretching vast and blue overhead. Jake works without a word, digging four graves side by side. Ed helps a little but rests quite often to regain his strength, as he should. The sound of the shovels cutting into the earth is unforgiving, each strike landing with a dull finality. I turn my face away. I can't watch them dig graves for people I loved.

Jake finishes the last grave and jumps out, dirt clinging to his sleeves and boots. He doesn't bother brushing it away.

The bodies are laid out gently yet simply. There is no finery, no ceremony beyond what we can manage. Jim and Constance look smaller than they did in life, as if the sickness hollowed them out even after it finished its work. Chuck and Glory, only ten and nine, lie between them. Tears fill my eyes for the lives they'll never get to live.

Ed stands beside Laurel, his arm tight around her shoulders. She is pale, eyes swollen, but she doesn't collapse. My knees are weak, but I will myself to stand tall, for my friends' sake.

Ed clears his throat and bows his head. His voice shakes, but he pushes through. "Dear Lord in Heaven, we thank you today for the lives of our friends, Jim and Constance, and their two sweet children, Charles and Gloria. We ask that you receive them into Your open arms with a love and peace we on Earth cannot imagine. Please give us the strength to go on without them, particularly their remaining children. Guide our hands as we tend to them. Let us never forget our friends who have perished and live our lives as a testimony to their love of You."

Amazing Grace pours from my lips without a thought, and Laurel joins in. As we begin the second verse, Jake lowers the bodies into the ground. Ed helps him cover the bodies with soil, which echoes out of the hole, dull and final, with each drop of the shovel. I turn away when Chuck and Glory are covered with earth. I don't trust my legs to hold me if I watch.

When it's done, four mounds rise from the ground. We place heavy stones on top of each grave to mark them until we can have proper grave markers made, and while we work, I release the guttural sobs I've been holding back. Jake wraps an arm around me in comfort, but nothing can contain the grief streaming from my body with every shoulder-wracking cry.

When the graves are covered and marked, we stand there a moment longer, none of us quite ready to leave. Eventually, we climb into the wagon, turning toward Andy's house, carrying the sorrow we can't leave behind, knowing the children are waiting, knowing the living still need us.

23

A BRIDGE ACROSS TIME

I stay by Joanna's side, watching her shoulders slump under the sorrow of everything we've seen, the grief clear in her eyes. I can't fix what's happened, can't bring Jim, Constance, or their children back, but I can be here for her. I vow to myself I will do anything to keep her safe, and to ease her pain however I can.

The first morning after the burials, I rise early, but Joanna is already gathering supplies: a beef and vegetable stew we made last night, as well as some clean blankets and cloths. We set out together toward Ed's house.

Joanna and I drop off fresh supplies, noting how much stronger the children look. Ed is worn out from helping with the graves yesterday, but he has color in his cheeks, and that is significant. We stay for a few moments, Joanna playing with the children, before heading to Andy and Kathleen's to help with their children and Jim's kids. They're all doing much better, even little Alice, who gave us a real scare when I found her not breathing.

The days slip by in a blur. I chop wood, boil water, begin to drain the well in preparation for repairing it, fetch herbs that might soothe stomachs, and guide Joanna as we nurse the last of the sick back to health. Her hands are comforting, her voice soothing when she sings to the children, but I can see the pain in her eyes and the way she struggles to hold back tears. I stay close, always ready to give her a hug or offer her an encouraging word or smile. I continue to let her see that she isn't carrying the loss alone.

By the end of the week, the children are up and playing. They're strong enough to play with the simple toys they have, and their eyes are clear for the first time in days. Jim's kids clearly miss their parents and their brother and sister, but every once in a while, they'll smile and laugh, and that makes my heart happy.

At home, Joanna constantly makes stew for the families, adding beans and more beef. I told her that would give them zinc, which will help them recover from cholera. She always makes sure each pot has enough for everyone. It's when I watch her caring for others that I come to the realization that I'm choosing to stay with her, with the life I've built here with her in 1875. The work, the loss, the victories we've fought for, and the choice comes easy: Even if I could, I wouldn't go back to my own time. I belong here with Joanna.

The sun drops behind the mesas. Joanna sits beside me on the porch, a tin cup of whiskey in her hands. I take a swallow from mine, feeling it burn, but I keep my eyes on her. She's so strong, smart, and damn beautiful. "I love you," I whisper, reaching over to take her hand.

"I know you do. I love you, too." She smiles at me, and warmth spreads through my chest.

It's time I told her the truth. "Listen, Joanna," I begin.

A sudden rattle of hooves on the dirt path steals our attention. Joanna stands, squinting. Two riders are coming up fast. One is an older man with gray hair, and the other is younger, dressed in a sharp suit. The younger man carries a small leather satchel. I rise instinctively, my muscles still wound tight from the day's work. The horses slow as they reach the edge of the yard.

The older man tips his hat. "Good evening. I'm Elias Morgan, an attorney from Mesilla, and this is Mr. Jonah Norton, a clerk of the court. We seek Miss Joanna Calloway." His tone is formal, and it carries authority.

Joanna raises an eyebrow, taking a tentative step forward. "I'm Joanna," she says. "What is this all about?"

Mr. Morgan dismounts as my heart threatens to leap out of my chest. Every step he takes feels like it could be the moment I'm accused of murdering Chase Sawyer. Mr. Morgan reaches into his satchel and pulls out a bundle of papers tied with string.

"We come with news concerning the Sawyer property. A few days ago, the body of Chase Sawyer was discovered in an old cabin north of here. He had no family members. There is no one to inherit his property, so it's about to be posted for sale. Given that your land borders it, we wanted to extend the offer to you. Are you interested in buying the Sawyer property, Miss Calloway?"

Joanna takes a breath. "I appreciate you gentlemen coming all the way out here to offer, but I don't want to buy it," she says. "However, I know some folks who might be interested."

The two men nod and hand over the papers, giving her a moment to glance them over. "Let's ride down the road a little way and ask the neighbors," she says.

The four of us ride toward Andy and Kathleen's place. When we arrive, Joanna knocks, and Kathleen appears first, wiping her hands on her apron, Andy close behind her, both smiling when they see us.

Joanna steps forward, explaining what the men from Mesilla said and suggests they might want it. Andy frowns thoughtfully, then nods, smiling with pride. "I've been saving to buy some land of my own," he says. "I would be glad to buy it. Thank you for thinking of us."

The lawyer hands him the papers, and Andy takes the pen offered, signing his name across the deed: *Logan Anderson.*

I freeze, and after catching my breath, ask, "Your name isn't Andy?"

"I go by Andy because my last name's Anderson," he replies.

Logan Anderson is my friend in 2025, and this man is his ances-tor. The land that will one day belong to Logan's uncle sits here now, in Andy's hands, a bridge across time I never thought I'd see. It's strange, and yet, damn touching to stand here and watch it all come together this way.

I glance over at Joanna. My instincts were right. It's time I told her the truth. She deserves to know who I really am and where I really came from. She deserves to fully understand me, and I can't hold it back any longer.

But for now, I stay quiet. I watch Andy and Kathleen smile, the sun fading behind them, the world feeling impossibly small and huge all at once.

When we return home, I get started on dinner. The scent of sizzling chicken and spices fills the kitchen. Joanna's in the other room, singing softly while mending one of her dresses.

I swallow hard. I've been circling this for weeks, trying to figure out the right words, and I know that tonight's the night.

"Dinner's ready," I call.

"It smells wonderful, Jake," she says as she enters. "Thank you for cooking tonight."

I set a plate at her place at the table, the candlelight dancing in her eyes as she sits. "I made your favorite," I say, trying for casual. "Fried chicken, roasted vegetables, and fresh bread." I take a seat opposite her, trying to calm the nerves knotting in my chest. I should just dive in.

"Thank you so much. I'm getting spoiled having a man like you to cook for me." She takes a bite, and the way she closes her eyes and tips her head back tells me I got it just right.

A few moments of silence pass between us as we enjoy our meal. But... I can't stay silent forever. "Joanna," I say, clearing my throat. "There's... something I need to tell you."

She tilts her head. "You sound so serious. What is it?"

I take a deep breath. "I'm not... just from Houston."

Her eyebrows knit together as her eyes roam my face. "You mean, you're not originally from Houston?"

I shake my head, forcing the words out. "I'm originally from Houston, but the year was 2025 last time I was there. I was born in 1997."

Joanna's eyes widen. She freezes, staring at me for a long moment before a laugh escapes her lips. "You're so silly, Jake."

I press on, knowing if I don't get it out now, I never will. "I'm serious, Joanna. I'm from the future. I know it sounds crazy, but it's true. And if you think about it a bit, you'll realize it makes sense."

She throws her head back and laughs. "Thank you, Jake. I needed that laugh tonight."

I lean forward, an edge of desperation in my voice. "I'm not joking. I can explain everything. I just need you to—"

She holds up a hand, cutting me off. Her lips press into a thin line. "Jake, look, I—" She shakes her head, words failing her. "I can't handle any more drama this evening. That's... that's not possible. You're pulling my leg, and I'm just too tired tonight."

My stomach drops. I want to grab her hand and make her see, but I don't want to push her away. She's too fragile right now. "Yeah, I know. I sound crazy. I'd think it was crazy if I heard it from someone else."

She looks down at her plate, pushing the food around like it suddenly tastes bitter. "Jake, I don't know why you're insisting on something so insane being the truth. But seriously, not tonight, all right?"

I nod slowly, trying to hide the ache. "Okay. I get it. I just wanted you to know the truth. Even if it's too much to take in right now."

She lifts her eyes to mine, searching, still skeptical. The moment stretches, and I know this isn't something she's going to easily accept. My secret is out, but the trust I hoped to build is already tangled in disbelief.

I swallow hard, reach for my whiskey, and force myself to hold back all the things I want to tell her.

She shakes her head again. "Did you hit your head? Do you need me to call for a doctor?"

"No, no. I'm fine. Just... never mind. It's not important. Not right now." I manage a soft smile. "Did I get the chicken right?"

She breathes a sigh of relief that I've changed the topic. "Yes, it's perfect."

"Good, good. I was afraid I cooked it too long." I lean back in my chair and watch her enjoy the meal. The truth's out, but she's not ready, and that's fine. I'll wait. One day, I'll make her understand.

2 4

FATE

Jake just told me he's from the future.

I don't know if he's joking or if he really believes it, but I can't wrap my mind around it. I can't seem to shake the words either. He sits there, his plate pushed aside, his face twisted in a frown, like my disbelief hurts him. Part of me is trying to brush it off, like it's just a bizarre statement for him to say to make me laugh, but the part that trusts him feels like there might be more truth to this than I want to admit.

We get up to clear the table, but I can't stop thinking about what Jake said. As I clear the plates and wipe down the table, my mind's elsewhere. I'm just trying to figure out why he'd say he was born one hundred and fifty years from now. Maybe the last few days, the illness and the deaths of our friends, have made him feel out of sorts.

I turn to him while I wash the dishes, my heart beating fast in anticipation of how he might respond. "Can you prove it?" I ask before I can stop myself. The words sound unintentionally rude, but they're out there now, and I can't take them back.

He arches an eyebrow and turns to look at me, holding my eyes. He gives a slight nod and then walks over to his pack and opens it. He walks over to the sink, holding out a small black tube. I've never seen anything like it before. There's a button on one end, and it looks strange and unfamiliar.

"This is a flashlight," he says, holding it up. "It's from the future." He clicks it on, and a beam of light cuts through the dim room.

I gasp, confused. "A flashlight?"

"Yes." He gives me a moment before continuing. "I used three of them to blind Sawyer while Jim shot him."

I look at the light, still in disbelief. "I don't... understand," I finally admit, my voice weak. "How can something like this exist?"

"I can explain it, but that's not all." He sets the light on the table and continues, pulling out another item and handing it to me. "This is something you won't see around here. It's packed with protein and lasts for years."

I turn it over in my hands. The wrapper has a lot of writing on it, but the words "protein bar" stand out to me. I don't even know what the wrapper is made of. I frown, unsure what to make of it. "What in the world is this?" I ask, my voice shaky. "Where did you get wrapping like this?"

"Open it," he says.

With a deep breath, I open the package and see that it's food, but certainly not anything I've ever seen before.

"Taste it," he says.

I smell the bar and take a bite. "Sweet Lord, this tastes terrible, Jake. Why would you eat this?"

He laughs. "We eat them in the future because they give us enough energy for our bodies to run on for hours."

I shake my head and set the offensive item down on the counter next to the sink.

He continues, pulling out a small bag with a bright blue wrapper and holding it up to the light. "These are what I gave Margot when she was hurt."

He hands me this bag, too. Again, the unusual packaging looks odd. This doesn't resemble anything from the stores I've seen around here. Maybe Houston has shops with wares contained in brightly colored wrappers like this, but it still feels completely out of place. I turn the bag over in my hands, still unsure. "What is it?"

"Dog treats," he explains, still digging in his bag. All this time, I've never looked in there. Now, I'm glad I haven't. I might've had a heart attack.

Jake pulls out the thermometer he used on the children. Before, I only saw it from a distance, but now that I'm looking closer, it's very strange. He taps a button, and the small screen flashes to life.

"See?" he says, holding it out to me. "It's digital. It takes a reading in seconds."

My mouth feels dry. "Digital? That thing is magic!" I can't help but blurt out, staring at the numbers on the tiny screen. The idea that such a thing exists is beyond anything I've ever imagined.

His claims are starting to make sense in some strange, impossible way. My head is spinning, but I can't turn away.

He looks me in the eye. "Come on, Joanna." His tone is light, with a hint of a challenge. "You must've noticed that my rifle's different."

I glance over at the rifle resting against the wall, the sight of it sending a little jolt through me, and I have to admit it's nothing like the guns we use around here.

"And Ace," he adds, nodding toward the black and white dog lying on the floor. "Have you ever seen a dog like him before?"

I already know the answer to that. I've never seen a dog like him, and I've thought about it many times, but now, along with everything else, I'm starting to wonder how Jake is from a place and a time I don't understand.

He looks at me, gauging my reaction, and I feel so dizzy and overwhelmed that I take a seat at the table. Then, he pulls something out of his pack that I can't even begin to explain. It's a small, black, smooth box, but unlike anything I've ever laid eyes on. He holds it up, and I stare at it, trying to make sense of what it could be.

"This," he says, "is a phone."

"A phone?" I echo with no clue as to what that means.

He holds down a tiny button, and the object suddenly glows.

I stare at it, every part of me rigid with shock and confusion. I grip the edge of the table, trying to remain calm, but I can't tear my eyes away. "How... how is this even possible?" I whisper, my voice trembling.

He smiles and squeezes my shoulder, trying to comfort me. "Don't be scared, Jonna. You know I'd never hurt you. In my time, we use this little box as a way to talk to people from anywhere in the world. It can do so many things, you wouldn't even believe it if I told you."

I think back to the past few months, to the way he knew exactly how to fix Jim's leg wound, how he stitched Margot and kept her from bleeding to death, how he treated the cholera when no one else had a clue. None of it should make sense, and yet it does. Maybe he really is from the future.

He stares at me for a long moment before speaking again, his voice low and full of intensity. "I didn't tell you all this to scare you. In fact, I hid it all as best I could so that I didn't alarm you, but I want you to know the truth. I want you to know who I am and where I'm from because, Joanna, I want to stay. I want to build a life here with you."

Waves of emotions crash over me as I realize that he's saying he'd give up everything: his life, his friends, his family, even his own time, just to stay here with me. He loves me enough to give up everything?

"I can't offer you much, Joanna," he continues. "I don't have land like you do. I don't have gold, status, or even a good reputation in town to get me started, but I love you. You have my loyalty, my hard work, and as long as you'll have me, I'm not going anywhere."

His words feel raw, real, and like they come from deep inside him. He's offering me his heart.

"I believe you," I whisper, standing. I wrap my arms around his neck and kiss him.

He kisses me back, his hands sliding around my waist, lifting me gently off the floor. I've never felt like this before. Love spreads through my chest in a wave of warmth I can barely contain. When the kiss ends, he looks into my eyes. "Joanna, will you marry me?"

I don't even have to think about it. "Yes!"

He beams, his eyes lighting up, and he grips my hands just a little tighter. "I love you," he says.

"I love you, too," I whisper as he kisses me again.

I never thought I'd meet a man who would give up everything for me. Yet, here we are, and it doesn't feel like a coincidence. It feels like fate. It feels like time itself has brought him to me—exactly when I needed him the most.

25

I DO

Joanna

The dress shop is crowded with women milling around, some discussing fabrics, others examining patterns, but it all feels a little overwhelming. I'm not one for crowds. I don't enjoy the noise and the bustle. Sometimes, the city shops are a bit too much for me, but today, I can't help but feel the flutter of butterflies in my stomach. I'm excited to be here, standing in the dress shop with Kathleen and Laurel, picking out my wedding dress.

Kathleen's already holding up bolts of cloth, as if she's trying to decide what shade of white would suit me best. "I thought this one might be nice," she says, gesturing to a delicate cream satin. "It'll look beautiful with your hair."

I take the fabric from her, feeling its smoothness between my fingers. It's soft and beautiful. I try to picture how it'll look on me. "It's lovely," I say, setting it aside. "But I think I want to keep looking."

Kathleen nods, her eyes warm with understanding. "Of course, we'll find something that feels just right." A reassuring smile parts her lips. She always knows how to make me feel better, even when I'm uncertain.

We move to another row of dresses, and I stare at the different fabrics. There are so many to choose from. Some are lace, some satin, some silk, and some are fabrics I'm not sure I recognize. Simple dresses hang on one side of the row, while more ornate gowns hang on the other. I try to picture each one on me, but none of them seem to fit the feeling I want for my special day.

Kathleen pulls a dress off a hook on the back wall. It's a simple gown with puffy sleeves and a soft, flowing skirt made of cotton. "How about this one?" She holds it up for me to see.

I step closer, taking in the dress. It's pretty, but something about it doesn't feel quite right. "It's beautiful," I say slowly, "but it's not exactly what I'm looking for."

Laurel, who has been quietly watching, speaks up from the side. "You're right," she says, her voice gentle but sure. "It's pretty and simple, but it doesn't have that spark you're looking for."

Kathleen nods, rehanging the gown. "I think you're right. Let's keep looking."

I feel a little relieved to hear them both agree. I don't want to settle for something just because it's pretty. I want to feel like myself in it, not like I'm wearing a costume.

We continue through the racks, and I start to feel like I'm getting closer. Then, one dress in particular catches my eye. The ivory fabric gleams softly in the light, and the lace sleeves are delicate, almost ethereal. The floral lace pattern spills from the sleeves across the bodice, intertwining with the low neckline in a way that feels both graceful and intimate. The skirt, made of satin and fine netting, falls gently to the floor, the layers shifting with the slightest movement, catching the light and seeming to float on their own. It's light, almost weightless, like it could carry me away. I can already see myself wearing it, standing next to Jake, and for the first time, I feel the certainty that this is the dress I was meant to wear.

"This one has your name written all over it," Laurel says, her voice full of approval.

I smile, feeling a surge of excitement. "I completely agree." I slip into the back room and pull the dress on. The moment I look in the mirror, I know this gown was made for me. It fits so well, the lace sleeves hugging my arms just right, and the elegance of the dress makes me feel both beautiful and comfortable. It's everything I've ever dreamt of. With just a few alterations, it will be perfect.

When I step out, Kathleen and Laurel both gasp. Laurel's eyes brighten as she looks me over. "You look stunning."

Kathleen smiles wide, clearly pleased. "It's perfect, Joanna."

I feel a rush of relief, a deep sense of peace settling over me. "I think this is the one," I say softly, my heart light. "It feels like it was waiting for me."

The dress shop owner comes over and makes a few pins, but I insist I'll make the few minor alterations at home. The dress is divine, and I don't want to let it out of my sight for one moment.

Now that we've settled on my dress, we shift our attention to dresses for Kathleen and Laurel, who will stand next to me. I already know what I want for Laurel. She needs something bold to match her sapphire blue eyes and chestnut brown hair, and I think a deep indigo will make both stand out. It doesn't take us long to find the perfect dress. It's striking, just like her.

As for Kathleen, her red hair and green eyes make her the perfect match for something in a rich forest green. We find a dress that brings out the warmth in her complexion and her fiery hair.

Both gowns will need some alterations, but we've got plenty of time for that, and the dressmaker is quite talented.

With the dresses picked out, I feel a sense of accomplishment. This wedding is truly happening–I'm really going to marry Jake. We still have some planning to do, but it's all coming together. My heart won't stop fluttering in my chest like I'm a schoolgirl. Jake is the most amazing man I've ever met, and he's about to be mine.

* * *

THE CHURCH WE'VE CHOSEN IN MESILLA IS SMALL, NOTHING LIKE THE grand ones I've read about in storybooks. It's simple, with worn pews and a wooden floor that creaks beneath our feet. I've always preferred places like this. It's quiet, unassuming, with the kind of energy that allows one to hope, feel, and breathe. There's no grand procession, no decorations that outshine the reason we're here. It's just the people we care about, gathered together in one place.

The morning of the wedding, I stand in the small room at the front of the church, the quiet buzz of the guests arriving seeping through the walls. The air smells of fresh wildflowers tied up in small bouquets for us to carry and the faint scent of lavender, which Kathleen and Laurel are tucking into my hair. We're all dressed, anxious for what's to come, and yet there's something peaceful about these last few moments.

Kathleen steps back. "I can't believe this day is finally here."

"I never thought it would come, either," I reply. "I never saw myself getting married, let alone to the love of my life."

She smiles. "I'm so glad the two of you found one another."

I bite back a laugh. If she only knew the truth….

Glancing over at the clock on the wall, I see that the ceremony is about to start, and I'm ready for what's next, ready to walk down that aisle toward Jake and to become his wife.

We go out into the vestibule, and Laurel opens the doors to the chapel. Jake stands at the altar, looking more handsome than ever in his dark suit. When his eyes meet mine, joy blooms through my entire body, head to toe. I'm about to marry the man who chose this life with me. Ed and Andy grin from next to him, both of them happy to see the two of us tie the knot.

Kathleen leans in to whisper, "You're ready."

The music begins, and my friends walk down the aisle. As they reach the front, everyone rises. Then, it's my turn. I take a deep breath and step forward, walking toward my destiny as Mrs. Joanna Rawlins.

At the front, I look up at Jake, biting my bottom lip. His eyes sparkle. He's never looked more handsome. "You look absolutely gorgeous," he whispers as he takes my hand, and Pastor Thomas begins the ceremony with a reading from 1 Corinthians. Then, it's time for us to share our vows with one another before God and our dearest friends.

Jake explained to me that in the future, the bride and groom will write their own special vows to one another. It's an idea I love and have embraced. After a prayer, the pastor nods for him to speak.

"Joanna, from the moment I met you," Jake begins. "I knew my life was about to change. I didn't know how, but I knew you were someone I couldn't walk away from. I promise to stand by you through every challenge, every moment of joy, and every quiet day in between. I will cherish you for the person you are and thank you for helping me to become the person I am today. I will love you with the same fierce loyalty I have always had for those I care about, but now, it's all for you. I will always protect you. Today, I give you my heart completely. You are my home, and I will spend every day of my life making sure you know you are loved, valued, and supported. I promise you this: No matter where life takes us, you'll never have to walk alone."

I wipe away a tear from my cheek, take a deep breath, and look into his eyes. "Jake, I promise to love you, even on the days when we don't have all the answers and when the road feels uncertain. I will be your partner in all things, your strength when you need it, your comfort when you're weary, and your laughter when the world feels too heavy. I vow to never take this love for granted, to never stop fighting for us, and to always choose you, day after day, year after year. I will share in your joys, help carry your burdens, and celebrate everything that makes us who we are. Together, we will build a future filled with love, trust, and respect. You are my heart, my home, and my forever. With you, I am complete."

Pastor Thomas looks at me. "Do you, Joanna Diane Calloway, take this man to be your lawfully wedded husband?"

I don't even hesitate. "I do."

"And do you, Jake Nathaniel Rawlins, take this woman to be your wife?"

"I do."

As Jake slides my mother's ring onto my finger, I think of our future together. Not the one I thought I would have, but the one we are about to create.

Pastor Thomas looks between us and says, "I now pronounce you husband and wife. You may kiss the bride."

Jake pulls me close, his hand resting gently on my cheek as he leans in. The kiss is soft but full of the promises of everything we've just vowed to each other.

As we kiss, the room erupts into applause. Everyone rises to their feet, cheering, their smiles wide, their joy genuine. A rush of warmth envelops me, the sound of their happiness surrounding us.

After the ceremony, everyone wants to congratulate us. They form a procession, hugging us and giving us their well-wishes. Clara has graciously offered to open her home for cake and dancing. Jake and I are excited to celebrate with all of our friends. I can hardly take my eyes off him.

As we step through the double doors of the church, on our way to our reception, hands intertwined, I can't help but beam.

2 6

HONEYMOON

After the reception, I change into a traveling gown and wave goodbye to our friends. Jake helps me into the seat, and we set out. The wagon bumps along the dusty road as we approach Las Cruces. The sun has started its slow descent behind the distant hills, painting the sky in rich hues of pink and purple.

When we roll into the city, I take in the sight of the bustling streets, the market, and the hustle of people walking between vendors. We cross the main street, pulling up in front of the finest hotel in town. The two-story brick building stands tall against the fading light.

Jake jumps down from the wagon and offers me his hand. "Shall we?"

I smile at him, stepping down into his waiting arms. "Lead the way."

Inside, the hotel is the grandest I've ever seen, with high ceilings and elegant furnishings. The scent of coffee and cigar smoke drifts through the air, adding a touch of home to the space.

We check in, and Jake gets the key, leading me upstairs. Our room is just as impressive as the lobby. There's a large, comfortable bed with crisp linens, a wooden dresser with intricate carvings, and a window that lets in the last of the daylight. It's everything we need. Just being here with Jake, knowing this is the start of our life together, feels perfect.

After unpacking, Jake takes my hand again, and we head out for dinner. The restaurant is down the street. Inside, the air smells of fresh baked bread. We sit at a small table near the back, the soft glow from a candle at the center of the table lighting up Jake's captivatingly handsome face.

He looks across at me, smiling. "This is really nice, isn't it?"

"It's perfect, Jake."

We eat our fill, savoring the food and the joy of celebrating our wedding–alone. Afterward, we stroll back to the hotel and hear a small band of musicians on the street corner, playing an upbeat tune.

Jake pauses, pulling me a little closer. "Want to dance?"

"Dance? Here?" I ask, a bit apprehensive.

"Sure. It'll be fun." He winks at me, and my stomach twists into a knot.

As the musicians play, the sound of the fiddle and guitar blending together, Jake pulls me close with a grin that lights up his whole face. He twirls me in the middle of the street, my feet momentarily lifting off the ground before I land back into his arms. We laugh together, spinning under the starlit sky, the music weaving around us like a dream. The world fades away, leaving just the two of us in this perfect, unexpected moment, dancing as if there's no tomorrow.

When we return to our hotel room, I slip into my prettiest night-gown, and Jake sheds everything except his undergarments. He seems to have been sculpted straight from a statue of a Greek god. I reach for him, laying my palms on his chest, savoring the rock hard muscle beneath them.

He looks at me with a hunger that makes my heart race. "Joanna?" His voice is deep and husky. "You're so stunning. All day, I've had to fight the urge to touch you."

I smile, a flush of heat spreading through my body. "I've been waiting for this moment, Jake. I want you to take me."

He steps closer, reaching out to cup my face. He leans in, his lips brushing against mine in a soft, tender kiss. I melt into him, my body pressing against his as the kiss deepens. His tongue explores my mouth, sending shivers down my spine.

His hands move down, tracing the curves of my body, his touch sending sparks of delight through me. He pulls away slightly, his eyes filled with desire. "I want to taste every inch of you, Joanna. I want to make you moan my name."

I gasp as his hands find the hem of my nightgown. He lifts it slowly, his eyes never leaving mine. The cool air of the room brushes against my bare skin as his hands roam over my body, his touch firm, exploring every inch of me.

He leads me to the bed, positioning himself so he's leaning over me, his lips trailing kisses over my hot skin, his tongue flicking out to taste me. I moan, my fingers tangling in his hair. His tongue delves deeper, and I pull him even closer, feeling how hard he is against my thigh.

"Jake," I moan as his lips find my neck. "That feels so good."

He pulls away to look up at me, a wicked grin on his face. "I love you so much, Joanna. I can't believe you're finally my wife."

He lifts his body, holding himself over me, and teases my breasts again. I reach out, my hands tracing the lines of his biceps, feeling the heat of his skin. "I want to feel you inside me, Jake," I whisper.

He positions himself at my entrance, his cock hard and ready, then pushes into me slowly, filling me completely. I scream with ecstasy, my whole body arching against his as he moves. His thrusts are slow and deep, each one sending waves of bliss through me. He grips my hips, driving me wild.

"You feel so good, Joanna," he groans.

I wrap my legs around his waist, pulling him deeper inside of me. His thrusts become faster and harder, each one driving me closer to the edge again. I can feel another orgasm building, the pleasure intensifying with each thrust.

"Jake," I gasp, my nails digging into his back. "I'm close. I'm so close."

He grinds against me, hitting just the right spot. I cry out as I come a second time. Jake fills me up again, thrusting deep and fast, pulsing as he spills inside of me.

He collapses beside me, and I turn to face him, struggling to catch my breath. He smiles, his eyes filled with love and satisfaction.

"That was incredible, Joanna," he says.

I laugh softly. "You're the one who did all the work." I rest my head on his chest, content to be in his arms.

As we lie there, wrapped in each other's arms, we know that this is just the beginning of our journey together, and I can't wait to explore it all with Jake by my side.

2 7

FAMILY

We've been newlyweds for a couple of months now, and it's starting to feel like we've been married forever, but in the best way. There's no second-guessing anymore. I'm here with Joanna, exactly where I'm supposed to be, and every day is a step forward in this exciting life we're sharing.

I'm up before the sun, like usual. The mornings are quiet, still, and full of possibilities. I sit out on the porch for a while, sipping coffee, watching the sky stretch from dark navy to purple, then pink, and finally blue. The ranch is still asleep, but I know it won't stay that way for long.

Joanna's always up with the sun, too, already starting breakfast and getting things done. I smile to myself and stand, stretching my arms over my head, and walk back inside to help.

After breakfast, we make our way to the barn. We feed the goats and chickens, milk the cows, take care of the dogs and the horses, and then it's time to check the herd.

By the time we finish, the sun is higher, beating down on us, but there's a satisfaction that comes with hard work. The cattle are where they need to be, and fences have been mended.

Joanna's already making plans for the future. "We'll need to drive the herd into the market again soon."

"You're always thinking ahead."

"Someone's gotta keep you in line and moving forward." She winks at me, and a fire lights low in my belly.

I pull her close for a moment. "You're the boss, Mrs. Rawlins. Whatever you need, I'm in."

She smiles, her eyes sparkling. "I know you are."

The day stretches out ahead of us, filled with more work, plans, and little moments that make this life worth living. There's still a lot to do, but there's nowhere I'd rather be.

Later in the evening, Joanna reminds me that we're supposed to head over to Andy and Kathleen's new place for dinner. I'm looking forward to the change of pace, especially after a full day of ranch work. We've been working hard, and the thought of sitting down to a meal with friends sounds like the perfect way to unwind.

We finish up our chores and clean up. The sky is turning a soft golden hue, the kind of light that makes everything look a little more tranquil. We climb into the wagon. The drive to Andy and Kathleen's is short.

When we approach their ranch house, children's laughter spills through the open window. They're probably running around like they always do. Andy's out front, moving some hay bales around, his sleeves rolled up and his face glistening with sweat. He waves as we pull in.

We get down from the wagon and head inside, one of the children holding the door open for us. He greets us, and I muss his hair until he jerks away. Kathleen's voice floats from the kitchen, mixing with the sounds of the kids playing. There's a certain kind of chaos in their home, but it's the kind of noise that feels comfortable and familiar.

"Hey there," Kathleen greets us as we step inside. She's carrying a tray of rolls that smell divine. "You're just in time for dinner."

"I brought a pie," Joanna says, holding it with one arm as she hugs her friend with the other.

"I'll put it in the kitchen." Kathleen thanks us and disappears for a moment.

The children swarm around us, excited to see us, their faces lighting up when Joanna hugs each of them. She's their favorite, of course. I watch them play and joke, the noise filling the house in a way that's almost deafening, but heartwarming all the same.

Before we sit down to dinner, Ed and Laurel arrive with their kids. We all squeeze around the table. The house fills with the sound of dishes being passed, the buzz of the children's laughter, and the warm hum of friendly chatter.

As we eat, the kids share stories about their day on the ranch, helping with the animals, working alongside Andy, and pitching in with chores. The older ones dive into talks about the new projects they're working on while the younger ones compete for attention, eager to share their own stories. I can't help but watch Joanna as she navigates it all, giving each of them her time and attention, no matter how chaotic the room gets. I always thought this was the time period when children were seen but not heard—but not in this house.

At one point, Ed looks over at Joanna with a sly grin. "So, are you still planning on a cattle drive comin' up soon?"

She nods. "Yes, we're keeping an eye on the market. Things are looking good, but I want to make sure we're ready before making any big moves."

"Sounds like a good plan," Ed agrees, taking a drink of his beer. "Just let me know when you need me."

The conversation moves from the cattle market to Andy and Kathleen taking over Sawyer's ranch and how much they enjoy the extra space with all these children. The kids chime in with compliments on the meal and ask for seconds. It's easy to forget the world outside when we're all together, laughing and talking about nothing and everything. This is the kind of night I've always wanted. I don't need fancy dinners or big events. It's these special moments with people we care about that really matter.

After we've all eaten our fill, the kids scramble outside to play. The sound of their voices echoes through the yard as we settle onto the porch, where the air has cooled and the stars are starting to appear. Other than the kids, the night is quiet except for the occasional chirp of a cricket and the rustle of the wind through the trees. It's peaceful here.

I glance over at Joanna next to me, her hand resting on my arm. Her eyes meet mine, and for a moment, it's like everything slows down. The work, the future, the uncertainty of life–it all fades away, leaving just the here and now.

"I'm glad we came," she says quietly. "It feels good to step away for a while."

"Yeah," I reply, squeezing her hand. "It's nice to be with family."

Joanna leans into me, and we sit there for a while in comfortable silence, watching the kids chase fireflies in the yard. The sky turns darker with each passing minute. The moon rises higher, casting a silver glow over the yard. Tomorrow will come with its own set of challenges, but for tonight, this moment is perfect. There's nowhere else I'd rather be.

When it's time to leave, we say our goodbyes, the kids hugging us tight before we head back to the wagon. The ride back to the ranch is calm, and as we pull up to the house, I feel a sense of pride wash over me. I'm proud to be a rancher in 1875. I'm proud to work hard and make a living, but most of all, I'm proud to be Joanna's husband.

We step inside, and I catch Joanna's eye. She smiles up at me, a contented expression that makes everything feel perfect. "We should try to make some children of our own," she says with a sly grin.

Laughing, I pull her close. "I'm game for that." I kiss her, and the world around us fades to black.

I'll never know if I could've gone back to 2025, but even if I had the chance, I wouldn't have even tried. That life, with all its comforts and familiarity, was something I once thought I wanted, but here, with Joanna, I've found what I was really searching for. This life—this love, this home—is real, and I'm exactly where I'm supposed to be. I wouldn't trade it for anything. Whatever the future holds, I'll face it here, with her by my side.

ALSO BY ID JOHNSON

Stand Alone Titles

All I Want for Christmas is Pooch

(*sweet contemporary romance*)

Christmas Memory

(*sweet contemporary romance*)

Meet Cute Me Under the Mistletoe

(*sweet contemporary romance*)

The Doll Maker's Daughter at Christmas

(*clean romance/historical*)

Pretty Little Monster

(*young adult/suspense*)

The Journey to Normal: Our Family's Life with Autism (*nonfiction*)

Found by the Alpha (*fantasy romance*)

Sweet As Maple Syrup series

Leaving Autumn

Cold Turkey

Snowed Inn

Love Throughout Time

(*time travel romance*)

Back to Titanic (free!)

Back to Gettysburg

Back to Bunker Hill

Back to the Highlands

Back to Port Royal

Back to the Inquisition

Back to Salem

Back to Plymouth

Back to Whitechapel

Back to the Old West (Jan 2026)

Back to the Ton (Feb 2026)

Back to the Crown (March 2026)

Back to Pompeii (April 2026)

Silverwood Academy

(paranormal romance)

Vampire Hunter (free!)

World Builder

Realm Jumper

Celestial Springs

(psychological thriller/literary fiction/women's fiction)

<u>Beneath the Inconstant Moon</u>

<u>The First Mrs. Edwards</u>

<u>Leaving Ginny</u>

The Motherhood

(dystopian romance)

<u>Rain's Rebellion (free!)</u>

<u>Rain's Run</u>

<u>Rain's Return</u>

Ashes and Rose Petals

(contemporary romance/retelling of Romeo and Juliet and Cinderella)

<u>Girl in the Attic (free!)</u>

<u>Girl From the Tomb</u>

<u>Girl On the Beach</u>

Nashville Country Dreams

(contemporary romance)

<u>Meant to Marry Me (free!)</u>

<u>Lead Me Home</u>

<u>You Are the Reason</u>

Forever Love series

(clean romance/historical)

<u>Cordia's Will: A Civil War Story of Love and Loss</u>

<u>Cordia's Hope: A Story of Love on the Frontier</u>

The Clandestine Saga series

(paranormal romance)

<u>Transformation (free!)</u>

<u>Resurrection</u>

<u>Repercussion</u>

<u>Absolution</u>

<u>Illumination</u>

<u>Destruction</u>

<u>Annihilation</u>

<u>Obliteration</u>

<u>Termination</u>

A Vampire Hunter's Tale (based on The Clandestine Saga)

(paranormal/alternate history)

<u>Aaron (free!)</u>

<u>Jamie</u>

<u>Elliott</u>

<u>Christian</u>

The Chronicles of Cassidy (based on The Clandestine Saga)

(young adult paranormal)

So You Think Your Sister's a Vampire Hunter? (free!)

Who Wants to Be a Vampire Hunter?

How Not to Be a Vampire Hunter

My Life As a Teenage Vampire Hunter

Vampire Hunting Isn't for Morons

Vampires Bite and Other Life Lessons

Gone Guardian

Death Does Not Become Her

Blood of the Vampire Hunter (based on The Clandestine Saga)

(paranormal romance)

Night Slayer (free!)

Shadow Stalker

Queen Catcher

Mother Hunter

Father Finder

Ghosts of Southampton series

(historical romance)

Prelude

Titanic

Residuum

Lusitania

Heartwarming Holidays Sweet Romance series

(Christian/clean romance)

Melody's Christmas (free!)

Christmas Cocoa

Winter Woods

<u>Waiting On Love</u>

<u>Shamrock Hearts</u>

<u>A Blossoming Spring Romance</u>

<u>Firecracker!</u>

<u>Falling in Love</u>

<u>Thankful for You</u>

<u>Melody's Christmas Wedding</u>

<u>The New Year's Date</u>

Charles Town Brides (based on Heartwarming Holidays Sweet Romance)

(Christian/clean romance)

<u>From This Moment (free!)</u>

<u>Can't Help Falling in Love</u>

<u>It's Your Love</u>

<u>When You Say Nothing At All</u>

<u>My Girl</u>

<u>Unchained Melody</u>

<u>I Only Have Eyes For You</u>

<u>At Last</u>

<u>The Very Thought of You</u>

Reaper's Hollow

(paranormal/urban fantasy)

<u>Ruin's Lot (free!)</u>

<u>Ruin's Promise</u>

<u>Ruin's Legacy</u>

When Kings Collide

(steamy historical romance)

<u>Princess of Silence</u>

Collections